DUST ACROSS THE RANGE

Dust Across the Range

MAX BRAND

A Black Horse Western

ROBERT HALE · LONDON

Copyright 1937 and 1938 by *The American Magazine*
Copyright renewed 1965 and 1966 by Dorothy Faust
First published in Great Britain 1994

ISBN 0 7090 5158 1

Robert Hale Limited
Clerkenwell House
Clerkenwell Green
London EC1R 0HT

Published by arrangement with
Golden West Literary Agency

Photoset in North Wales by
Derek Doyle & Associates, Mold, Clwyd.
Printed and bound in Great Britain by
WBC Ltd, Bridgend, Mid-Glamorgan.

DUST ACROSS THE RANGE

ONE

Off the high, level plateau of the range, cattle trails dip like crooked runlets of white water into the valley of the Chappany. Louise Miller, bound for home on her best horse, came off the level like a ski jumper from the take-off mound. She had come back to the ranch to celebrate her twenty-first birthday and take over the management of the 40,000-acre spread while her father embarked on a two-year drifting voyage through the Old World.

She had brought home in her pocket, so to speak, two specimens of man between whom she was to select a husband, because, as her father warned her, 'ranch days can be kind of long,' and she had ridden out alone on this day to think over the two of them and make her choice. She had made her decision and, having arrived at it, she was homebound, hell-bent, to tell big Frederick

7

Wilson that in the pinch he was man enough to suit her.

That was why she took the second downward bend of the trail so fast that Hampton skidded under her. Then the danger flashed in her eyes in the form of a three-stranded barbed-wire fence, as new and bright as a sword out of a sheath. She sat Hampton down on his hocks and skidded him to a halt a yard or so from the wire.

A hundred yards away nine men were building a second line of fence, stretching and nailing wire, or tamping new posts in place, or screwing augers into the hard ground. Eight of them were CCC men, she knew, donated by the government to help make the Hancock ranch an example of soil-conservation methods to the entire range. The ninth man, pinch-bellied and gaunt-ribbed from labor, was undoubtedly the fellow to blame for this pair of insane fences which cut the old trail like a pair of knives. He worked with a thirty-pound crowbar, breaking the hardpan.

That was Harry Mortimer, who for two years had been at work trying to make the Hancock place pay real money. He had a one-third share in the property and came out of the East with a brain crammed full of college-bred agricultural theory and an odd missionary desire to teach the ranchers new ways with the old range.

His family had spent long generations wearing down the soil of a New England farm until the bones of the earth showed through. Mortimer's father left the farm, went into business that prospered, but left his son the old yearning to return to the soil. That was why agriculture had been his study in college, but when he looked for a sphere to work in after graduation, the rocky little New England farms seemed too small a field. That was why he had gone to the West to exploit his inherited share in the Hancock place.

Whatever the bookish idiocy that suggested this pair of fences to him, Louise Miller wanted to get to him fast and tell him what she thought of the idea. So she hurried Hampton around the lower end of the fence. But here the ground chopped into an ugly 'badlands' of little gullies and gravel ridges. Hampton began to go up and down over them like a small boat in a choppy sea. He slipped on loose soil. And the next instant Louise Miller was sailing toward the far horizon.

It never would have happened except that she was thinking about steering the chestnut, not keeping her seat. Her only thought was to damn everything, including her own folly and Harry Mortimer. Then she was sitting up, with the landscape settling back from a dizzy whirl. Sweating men were lifting her by the armpits, but Harry Mortimer was not among them. He had let this chip fall where it might while he climbed on one of the mules that grazed near the wagonload of posts and wire, and trotted off in pursuit of

Hampton.

Vaguely she heard the CCC men speaking words of concern and comfort and felt their hands brushing her off carefully, but she was mainly concerned with wishing Hampton would kick a pair of holes through Mortimer. Instead, the thoroughbred stood near the fence like a lamb and allowed himself to be caught and brought back at the mildest of dogtrots. Harry Mortimer dismounted from his mule and handed the girl the reins.

'I thought for a minute you might have a long walk home,' he said.

It was hard for her to answer, so she looked him over and pretended to be catching her breath. He worked stripped to the waist, with a rag of old straw sombrero on his head. The sun had bronzed him; sweat had polished the bronze. He had the light stance of a sprinter, but around his shoulders the strength was layered and drawn down in long fingers over his arms. The pain of labor and the edge of many responsibilities seamed his face, but above all he had the look of one who knows how to endure, and then strike hard.

At last she was able to say, 'Sorry you ran out of places where fences are needed. This is just some practice work for you and your men, I suppose? Or did you think it would be fun to block the trail and cut up the livestock on your barbed wire?'

He picked up the thirty-pound crowbar and tossed it lightly from hand to hand.

'While you're thinking up an answer,' said Louise Miller, 'I'd suggest that there's lots of fence to put up on my place, and where it will do good.... Where does the fun come in, Harry? Digging the holes or seeing the pretty wire flash in the sun?'

The CCC men laughed, heartily. She understood that they lived in almost religious awe of their boss, but they stood back and laughed with deep enjoyment.

'Talk it up to her, Chief,' they called. 'Don't lay down in the first round.'

'You have to give a lady the first hold, boys,' said Mortimer, grinning at them. Then he added, 'Any sore places from that fall, or are you just feeling sour?'

'Not at all,' said the girl, laughing with pure excess of hate. 'I'm simply asking a few questions.'

'Want me to answer pretty Lou Miller?' he asked. 'Or am I talking to the manager of the John Miller ranch?'

'I'm going to manage it, all right,' she nodded.

'D'you know enough to?' he demanded.... 'You fellows get back to that fence-line, will you?'

They departed, their grinning faces turned to watch the comedy.

'Every Miller who ever was born knows enough to run a cattle ranch,' she answered.

'By divine right, or something like that?' said Mortimer. 'Then why don't you know why I'm running these fences?'

11

'I do know. It's for exercise, isn't it?'

He jabbed the crowbar into the ground and leaned on it, smiling. But she knew that if she had been a man his fist would have been in her face.

'How long has the trail run over this ground?' he asked.

'Two or three years.'

'Where was it before?'

'Over there,' she answered, proud of her exact knowledge. 'Over there where those gullies are opening up.'

'Was there a trail before that one?'

'Yes. It traveled along that big arroyo.'

'What made the gullies and what started the big arroyo washing?' he asked her.

'Why, God, I suppose,' said the girl. 'God, and the rain He sent. What else?'

'It was the trail,' said Mortimer. 'It wore down through the grass and down through the topsoil till it was a trench, and the first heavy rains began to wash the trench deeper. I'm building these fences to turn the downdrift and the updrift of the cattle from the tanks. I'm making them wear new trails.'

She saw the justice of what he said. She saw it so deeply she was angered to the heart because she could find no good retort.

'The point is that the old range and the old range ways aren't good enough for you, Harry. Isn't that the point?'

12

She waved her hand across the valley of the Chappany to the house of her father and the green lake of trees that washed around it, and to the miles of level ground that spread beyond.

'The other generations didn't know. Is that it?' she asked, sharpening her malice with a smile.

He considered her for a moment, as though he doubted the value of making an answer. Then he pointed.

'See the edge of that thousand acres of hay your father planted?' he asked. 'And, spilling into the valley below it, you see the silt that's flowed onto the low ground? That silt spoils fifty acres of good river-bottom that's fit for the plow. Know how it comes to be there?'

'Wash from a heavy rain, I suppose?' she answered gloomily.

'Yes. Your father ripped up a thousand acres of virgin range land. His plow cut through the roots of the grass of the topsoil that's been accumulating for a million years. The rain came on the loose ground and washed the cream of it away. The first dry season and hard wind that comes along, and that thousand acres will blow away like feathers; and the earth will have a million years of work to do all over again.'

'Father had to have extra hay,' said the girl. 'That's why he planted. What else was he to do?'

'Look down the Chappany along the Hancock land,' said Mortimer.

13

'It looks like a crazy quilt,' she answered.

'Because it's strip-plowed to leave a percentage of holding grass; and it's contour-plowed in other places to keep the soil from washing. Those brush tangles in the gullies are dams that will keep the gullies from deepening. Every slope of more than twenty per cent is planted to trees; every slope of more than twelve goes to permanent grass. In another year or so I'll have every acre of the Hancock place buttoned down to the ground with grass or trees, so that it *can't* blow.'

'I understand,' she said. 'You've been reading the silly newspapers about dust storms. Do you happen to know that there's never been a dust storm on this range?'

'There *will* be, some day,' he answered. 'Look at the mountains, yonder. That blowing mist isn't clouds. It's dust. It's ten thousand acres going to hell this minute!'

She stared toward the horizon and, above the blue of the mountains, saw a smudging darkness in the air. Mortimer was saying, 'That's the Curtis Valley blowing up in smoke. A dry season and a strong wind.... Here's the dry season with us, well enough. The Chappany has stopped flowing, though it's only May. Realize that? Only May, and the range is bone-dry.'

She glanced down the slope at the lakes in the bottom of the valley. There were five of them extended by old dams. Three lay on her land; two belonged to the Hancock place. As a rule the Chappany ran for eleven months in the year, only ceasing in August, and during that month the cattle came in from miles off the dry back of the range. This year, to be sure, was very different, for as the little river ceased flowing, the water holes on the farther range also were drying up and the cows had already commenced to voyage to the valley for drink. Little wind-puffs of white spotted the tableland and drifted down into the valley as parched cattle came at a trot or a lope for the water. Scores of them even now stood shoulder deep in the lakes, and the throngs were lying on the dry shore waiting to drink again, and again, before they started the trek toward the back country and the better grass again.

Mortimer was pointing again. 'A dry season, and a hard wind,' he said. 'That thousand acres your father plowed is a gun pointed at the head of the entire country. If that starts blowing, the top-soil all over the range is apt to peel off like skin.... I tell you, every plow furrow on the range is like a knife cut; it may let out the life and leave you worthless dry bones. The whole range — beautiful damned miles of it – go up in smoke. My land lies right under the gun.'

Her brain rocked as she listened and felt conviction strike her as with hands. If she could not argue, at least she could hate. Her father hated this man, and she would have felt herself untrue to her name if she did not hate him in turn.

'And that was why you tried to stab Father in the back?' she asked.

'I complained to the government and the soil-conservation authorities,' he said. 'I did it after I'd tried a thousand times to talk sense to John Miller.... And they would have *made* him toe the line, except he knew the right political wires to pull.'

She laughed through her teeth. 'Wire-pulling? That's better than rope-pulling, Harry!' she said.

'You mean your father would like to see me lynched?' he answered. 'I suppose he would ... he hates me. I despise him.... But I'll tell you what I'd do. If I thought I could change his mind, I'd crawl a hundred miles on my hands and knees and kiss his feet. I'd sit up and beg like a dog ... because he's the king of the range and, until he wakes up, the whole range will remain asleep ... and one night it'll blow away.'

She swung suddenly into the saddle. This strange, savage humility troubled and stirred her so that it was hard to find in her heart the chord of hatred on which she had been strumming. The only answer she found was to say, 'Why not try him again, Harry? This evening, for instance. There's going to be a barbecue, and perhaps he'd be glad to see you. I'm sure the *boys* would be glad.

16

And so would I!' She laughed again, put some of her anger into her spurs, and made beautiful Hampton race like a long-gaited rabbit, scurrying down the slope....

Into the wagon Mortimer loaded his eight men at noon and drove the wagon back to the Hancock ranch house. He had been a fool, he told himself, to talk to the girl with a frank sternness, as though she were a man. He could not force a young wildcat like her to see the truth, but he might have tried to flatter her into a new point of view.

A dangerous expedient suggested itself to him now, and in that light of danger he began to see again the faces and the souls of the eight men in the wagon behind him. Every one of them had been with him at least a year and a half. Every man of them was like another right hand to Mortimer. They had come to him as a surly, unwilling, random collection which he had begged, borrowed, and stolen from the CCC camp at Poplar Springs, justified by his intention of making the Hancock ranch an exemplar in soil conservation to the entire range; but the entire eight had remained like members of a family. He gave them his time like water and they gave him back their ungrudging affection. He knew the worst that was in them and they understood his affection. They understood his ultimate purpose, also, which was far more than simply to put the

17

Hancock ranch on a high-paying basis: He wanted to reform the ranching methods of the entire range and widen the margin of security which old-fashioned methods constantly diminished.

Each one of the eight had some useful quality, some weakness. Baldy Inman was the most docile of all, but when he went on a binge, once a month, Mortimer sat with him night after night and brought him home again to sobriety. Bud McGee loved battle, and twice Mortimer had dragged him out of saloon brawls at the risk of both their necks. George Masters loved poker and knew all too well how to deal. Chip Ellis and Dink Waller were always about to start for the gold lands of Alaska and talked up the beauties of far countries till the rest of the boys were on edge. Lefty Parkman had been in the ring and he helped on Sundays teaching the boys to box. He had beaten Mortimer to a pulp, in spite of his lighter weight, Sunday after Sunday, until sheer dint of pain taught Mortimer the science and gave him a deadly left of his own. Pudge Major supplied music and noisy jokes.

Jan Erickson, the giant of the crew, had once broken away and followed the old call of the underworld as far as Denver, where Mortimer overtook him and brought him home again. Mortimer returned from that journey with an eye which changed gradually from black to purple to green, and Erickson's face was swollen for a

18

month, but they never referred to what happened in Denver and remained as brothers together in the times of need.

It was while he thought of his crew, one by one, that the determination to take the great chance came strongly home in Mortimer. He stopped the wagon in front of the big shed which had been turned into a barracks for the CCC workers. Shorty, the cook, was already in the doorway banging a tin pan and yelling to them to come and get it. Mortimer, instead of going in with them to sit at the long table, passed into the Hancock house.

As usual, he found Charlie Hancock stretched on the couch in the parlor with the limes, the sugar, the Jamaica rum, and the hot-water jug conveniently on the table beside him. Because of the heat of the day he was dressed in trunks and slippers only, and he had a volume of Boswell's *Johnson* propped on the fat of his paunch. His glasses, his prematurely aged face, and his short gray mustache gave him the air of a country gentleman reposing in a Turkish bath.

This posture of reading had become hardly more than a posture recently, for, since Mortimer had appeared and was willing to take charge of the ranch, Charles Hancock had sunk into a long and vicious decline. A fine education had given edge to one of the clearest minds Mortimer had ever met; it was also the most vicious brain he

19

knew. The main direction of the ranch work had been left to Mortimer, but there still remained on the place half a dozen haphazard cowpunchers whom Hancock picked up, not so much because they knew cows as because they shot straight and were devoted to him. Aside from rum and books, guns were the main preoccupation of Hancock. If he left his rum bottle, it was generally to go hunting with some of his harum-scarum hired men. They did not mix with the CCC men.

'Wang!' called Hancock. 'Bring another glass for Mr. Mortimer, and some more hot water.'

The Chinaman appeared in the kitchen door-way, bowed, and trotted off.

'I'm not drinking,' said Mortimer.

'Still a slave to conscience, Harry?' said Hancock.

Mortimer began to pace the room, on one side staring out a window that looked up the valley of the Chappany where he had worked so hard during the two years, on the other looking vacantly at the photograph of old Jim Hancock, who had retired from the ranch to live in a cottage in Poplar Springs. On $50 a month he kept himself happy with frijoles and whisky and let the world wag on its way. The literal arrangement was that the income from the ranch should be split three ways, one to old Jim, one to his son Charles, one to Mortimer; but as a matter of fact Charlie managed to use most of his father's portion besides his own.

'Yes,' said Charles Hancock, answering his own

question, 'a slave to the conscience that forces you to make the world a better place to live in. You see nothing but green, Harry. You want nothing but a big range and nothing but green on it. What is there you wouldn't do for it?'

'I've been wondering,' said Mortimer, vague with thought.

'Grass for cows, grass for cows!' said Hancock, laughing. 'And yet you'd die to give it to 'em.'

'It's something else,' answered Mortimer, shaking his head. 'It's the idea of a living country instead of a dying one.... Tell me, Charlie: What would happen if I showed my face at the Miller barbecue this evening?'

Hancock sat bolt upright, then slowly lowered himself back to the prone position. He took a deep swallow of punch. 'Nothing,' he said. 'Nothing ... at first.'

'And then?' asked Mortimer.

'At first,' said Hancock, smiling as he enlarged his thought, 'there would be a dash of surprise. Old John Miller wouldn't faint, but he'd come close to it. And his cowpunchers would have to remember that the whole range had been asked to see Lou Miller's twenty-first birthday.... Afterward, when the drink began to soak through their systems and got into their brains ... that would be different. I don't know just how it would happen. Someone would stumble against you, or trip over your foot, or find you laughing in his face and take

21

a word for an insult, or misunderstand the way you lifted an eyebrow … and presently you'd be stuck full of knives and drilled full of bullet holes!'

'You think Miller wants me dead as badly as that?' asked Mortimer.

'Think? I know! You bring down a damned commission on top of him. It rides over his land. It finds that the great John Miller has been overstocking his acres, destroying the grass with too many hoofs. The commission is about to put a supervisor in charge of the Miller ranch and cause all the Millers to rise in their graves. Only by getting a governor and a couple of senators out of bed in the middle of the night is he able to stop the commission…. And he owes all that trouble to you. Trouble, shame, and all. Wants you dead? Why, John Miller's father would have gone gunning for you in person, with a grudge like that. And John Miller's grandfather would simply have sent half a dozen of his Mexican cowboys to cut your throat. These Millers have been kings, Harry, and don't forget it.'

'Kings … kings,' said Mortimer absently. 'The girl will be running the place in a few days. And she's as hard as her father.'

'Soften her then,' said Hancock.

'She challenged me to come to the barbecue,' said Mortimer. 'If I come … will that soften her?'

'Of course it will,' answered Hancock. 'And the guns will soften *you*, later on. Are you going to be fool enough to go?'

'If I win her over,' said Mortimer, 'I win over the whole range. If the Miller place uses my ideas, all the small fellows will follow along. If I go to the silly barbecue, maybe it will make her think I'm half a man, at least. You don't hate a thing you can even partly respect.'

'Ah,' said Hancock. 'He's a noble fellow. Ready to die for his cause, and all that ... You bore me, Harry. Mind leaving me to my rum punch?'

Mortimer went out into the shed that housed the CCC men and passed through the room where the eight sat with a platter of thin fried steaks rapidly disappearing from their ken.

'Hi, Chief,' said Pudge Major. 'Are you giving me your share?'

'He can't eat ... the Miller gal fed him up to the teeth,' suggested Chip Ellis.

'He's lovesick,' shouted Bud McGee. 'You can't eat when you're lovesick!'

They all were shouting with laughter as he passed them and entered the kitchen, where Shorty was stubbing about on his wooden leg, laying out his own meal on a table covered with heavy white oilcloth.

'Hi, Chief,' he said. 'Can't you chew a way through one of those steaks?'

'What's the lowest a man can be?' asked Mortimer, sitting on the window sill.

'Cabin boy on a South Seas tramp,' answered

Shorty instantly.

'How about a man who tells a girl he loves her? Makes love and doesn't mean it?'

'You take it with gals, and the rules are all different,' said Shorty. 'Now, over there in Japan ...'

'A white girl, Shorty, as straight as a ruled line, even if she's as mean as a cat.'

'Why, if a gal is straight and a gent makes her crooked ... why, they got a special place in hell for them, Chief,' said Shorty.

'Reasons wouldn't count, would they Shorty?' asked Mortimer.

'There ain't any reasons for spoiling a clean deck of cards,' said Shorty.

Mortimer went back into the dining-room and took his place at the head of the table. He speared a steak and dropped it on his plate. 'There's no work this afternoon,' he said.

'Quit it, Chief!' protested huge Jan Erickson. 'You mean you declare a holiday?'

'I'm going to a party, myself,' said Mortimer, 'and I've never asked you to work when I was off playing, have I?'

'Where's the party?' asked Pudge.

'Over the hills and far away,' said Mortimer....

He spent the early afternoon preparing himself with a scrubbing in cold water; then he dressed in rather battered whites, climbed into the one-ton truck, and prepared to deliver himself at the barbecue.

Charles Hancock appeared unexpectedly in the doorway of the ranch house, a fat, red, wavering figure. He called out, 'If you want to take that Miller girl into camp, you'd better slick yourself up with a five-thousand dollar automobile. You can't go fast enough in that contraption. She'll keep seeing your dust.'

Mortimer looked at his partner for a moment in silent disgust and silent wonder; then he drove off through the white heat of the afternoon.

When he bumped across the bridge and finally rolled up the trail onto Miller land, he felt that he had crossed the most important Rubicon of his life. Others were coming in swaying automobiles, in carts and buggies, and above all on mustangs which had cruised from the farthest limits of the range, but he knew that he would be the most unexpected guest at the carnival. Halfway up the slope the swinging music of a band reached him. He felt, in fact, like a soldier going into battle as he reached the great arch of evergreens which had been built over the entrance to the Miller grounds.

Sam Pearson, the Miller foreman, ranged up and down by the gate giving the first welcome to the new arrivals, and the first drink out of a huge punchbowl which was cooled in a packing of dry ice. When he saw Mortimer, the foreman came to a pause on a ready-made speech of welcome and stood agape with the dripping glass of punch in his hand. Then he came slowly up to the side of the truck and narrowed his eyes at Mortimer as though he were searching for game in a distant horizon.

'What kind of legs have you got to stand on, Mortimer?' he asked. 'What you think is gunna hold you up all through the day?'

'Beginner's luck,' said Mortimer.

The foreman suddenly held out the glass. 'Have this on me,' he said. 'You got so much nerve I wish I liked you.'

Mortimer drove on into the space reserved for parking, between the corrals behind the house. There he climbed slowly down to the ground and went on toward the Miller residence, with a sense that his last bridge, his last way of retreat had been broken behind him.

The crowd gave him some comfort in the feeling that he might lose himself among the numbers who drifted beneath the trees surrounding the ranch house. Throngs of colored lanterns swung from the lower branches and the gala air helped a sense of security, also. But he was noticed at once. A rumor ran ahead of him on invisible feet. A whisper spread, and heads were continually turning, amazed eyes were staring at him.

He put on an air of unconcern, but the weight of a man-sized automatic under his coat was the sort of companionship he wanted then.

26

It was Louise Miller whom he kept an eye for as he wandered casually through the crowd. He went down by the big open-air dance floor, where the band played and where a ring had been built for the wrestling and boxing which were to be part of the entertainment; but she was not there. He passed back to the open glade, where a huge steer was turning on a great spit against a backing of burning logs. For three generations the Millers had barbecued their meat in this manner for their friends, but roast beef was only one dish among many, for in enormous iron pots chickens and ducks were simmering, and in scores of Dutch ovens there were geese, saddles of venison, and young pigs roasting. There were kegs of beer and ale, kegs of whisky, incredible bowls of rosy punch, and such an air of plenty as Mortimer had never looked on before.

He lingered in the central scene of the barbecue too long and as he turned away he saw a pair of big cowpunchers, dressed up as gaily as Mexicans, solidly barring his way and offering fight as clearly as boys ever offered it in a schoolyard. Mortimer side-stepped them without shame, and went on, with their insulting laughter in his ears. He knew without turning his head that they were following him. Men began to be aware of him from both sides and from in front. He heard derisive voices calling out: 'The land doctor!' 'Give him a start home!' 'Help him on his way!'

He shrugged his shoulders to get the chill out of his spinal marrow. He made himself walk slowly to maintain a casual dignity, but he felt his neck muscles stiffening. When he stumbled on an uneven place, an instant guffaw sounded about him, and he felt as though a great beast were breathing at his shoulder. It was in the crisis of that moment that he saw a girl coming swiftly through the crowd, and saw Louise Miller panting with haste as she came up to him.

'Are you crazy – coming here?' she demanded.

'I thought you asked me,' said Mortimer.

'Come back to the house with me. I've got to talk with you and get you away,' she said. 'I've never heard of anything so idiotic. Didn't you see them closing in around you like wolves for a kill?'

'Just a lot of big, harmless, happy boys,' said Mortimer, and she glanced up sharply to see the irony of his smile.

They came through the trees to the wide front of the old house, and then through the Spanish patio, under the clumsy arches, and so into the house. She led him into a library. A vague, indecipherable murmur of voices sounded through the wall from the next room, but the girl was too intent on him to notice the sound.

'Sit down here,' she commanded. 'I'll walk around. I can't sit still.... Harry Mortimer, listen to me!'

He lighted a cigarette as he leaned back in the

28

chair and watched her excitement.

'It isn't my fault that you've come, is it?' she asked. 'You know it wasn't a real invitation, didn't you? Ask you up here into a den of wildcats? You knew that I didn't intend that!'

'What *did* you intend, then?' he asked.

She pulled up a chair opposite him, suddenly, and sat down on it, with her chin on her fist, staring at him. The billowing skirt of her dress slowly settled around her. 'You know,' she said. 'Those fences … the silly fall I took … and then I wasn't making very good sense when I argued; and it was a sort of crazy malice, to have the last word, and leave a challenge behind me. Ah, but I'm sorry!'

The lowering and softening of her voice let him look at her deeply for an instant.

'I'm not sorry,' he told her. 'D'you see? I'm here in the castle of the baron – right in the middle of his life. Perhaps he'll listen to reason now.'

'Because he can see that you're ready to die for your cause? No, he'll never listen! He's as set as an old army mule, and as savage as a hungry grizzly. He's in there now, Harry, and I've got to get you away before he –'

Here the door at the side of the room opened and the deep, booming voice of John Miller sounded through the room, saying, 'We'll announce Lou's engagement to you before the evening's over, Fred.'

'But, Mr. Miller, if we hurry her ...' said a big, handsome fellow in the doorway, as blond as Norway and built like a football tackle.

'She's made up her mind, and that's enough for me,' declared John Miller, leading the way into the library.

His daughter and Mortimer were already on their feet. In her first panic she had touched his arm to draw him away, but he refused to avoid the issue; the two of them stood now as though to face gunfire. It opened at once. John Miller, when he made out the face of Mortimer, ran a hand back through the silver of his long hair and grew inches taller with rage. He actually made a quick step or two toward Mortimer before another thought stopped him and he remembered that no matter who the man might be, he was a guest in the Miller house. He had the blue eyes of a boy and they were shining with a pair of bright, twin devils when he came up and took the hand of Mortimer.

'Mr. Frederick Wilson, Mr. Mortimer,' he said. 'I am happy ... a day when everyone ... I see, in fact, that you and Louise are old friends?'

He was in a sweat of white anger, though he kept himself smiling. Frederick Wilson, who could not help seeing that something was very wrong, looked quizzically from his fiancée to Mortimer.

'I'm sorry that I was here when you wanted to be private,' said Mortimer, withdrawing.

30

'Ah, about that!' exclaimed Miller. 'But I can trust you not to spread the word in the crowd? I want to save it as a surprise.'

Mortimer was already close to the door and, as he turned to go through it, he heard the girl exclaiming, 'But an announcement!'

'Have you two minds or one?' answered her father. 'If you have only one, it's already made up.... Now, what in the devil is the meaning of Mortimer here in my house, when the poisonous rat has been doing everything he can to ...'

Mortimer was already out of earshot and walking slowly down the hall, through the patio, and once more into the woods of the carnival, with the music of the band roaring and booming in his ear.

He was not noticed immediately, and he tried to interest himself in the variety of the people who had come to the barbecue, for they included every type, from tough old-timers whose overalls were grease-hardened around the knees, to roaring cowpunchers from all over the range and white-class citizens of Poplar Springs.

Near the glade where the roasting ox hissed and spat above the fire, he saw a compacted group that moved through the crowd like a boat through the sea, and a moment later he recognized the lofty, blond head of Jan Erickson! They were there, all eight of them, and they gathered around him now with a shout and a rush.

31

He took Pudge Major by the lapels of his coat and shook him. 'You're behind this, Pudge,' he said. 'You're the only one who could have guessed where I was coming. Now, you take the rest of 'em and get out of here. D'you know that every man jack in this crowd is heeled? And if trouble starts they'll shoot you boys into fertilizer.'

'And what about you?' asked Pudge.

'I'm having a little game,' said Mortimer.

'Yeah, and when you're tagged, you'll stay "it",' answered Dink Waller. 'We'll just hang around and make a kind of a background so's people will be able to see you better.'

'Listen to me. I'm ordering you back to the Hancock place,' commanded Mortimer.

This seemed to end the argument. They were looking wistfully at their chief when George Masters exclaimed, 'This is time off. Your orders ain't worth a damn this afternoon, Chief. We're where we want to be, and we're going to stay.'

With a half-grinning and a half-guilty resolution they confronted Mortimer, and he surrendered the struggle with a shrug of the shoulders; but already he felt, suddenly, as though he had walked with eight sticks of dynamite into the center of a fire.

A thundering loud-speaker called the guests to the platform entertainment, a moment later, and that invitation called off the dogs of war from Mortimer and his men. They drifted with the others toward the dance floor, and from the convenient slope Mortimer looked on with anxious, half-seeing eyes at dancers doing the buck and wing, at a competition in rope tricks, at a pair of slick magicians, at wrestlers, at a flashy bit of lightweight boxing, at an old fellow who demonstrated how Colts with their triggers filed off were handled in the old days. And still he was wondering how he could roll his eight sticks of dynamite out of the fire, when a huge, black-chested cowpuncher got into the ring to box three rounds with a fellow almost as tall and robed from head to foot with a beautiful coverage of muscles. The blond head of the second man meant something to Mortimer and, when the fellow turned, he recognized the handsome face of Frederick Wilson, smiling and at ease with the world.

The reason for his confidence appeared as soon as the gong was struck and the two went into action.

'He's got a left, is what that Wilson's got,' said Lefty Parkman. 'He's got an educated left, and look at him tie it onto Blackie's whiskers!'

The big cowpuncher, full of the best will in the world, rushed in to use both hands, as he had done many a time in saloon brawls, always to bump his face against a snapping jab. When he stood still to think the matter over, he lowered his guard a trifle, and through the opening Frederick Wilson

33

cracked a hammer-hard right hand that sagged the knees of the man from the range.

'What a sock!' said Lefty Parkman, rubbing his greedy hands together. 'But Blackie don't know how to fall!'

The cowboy, though his brains were adrift, still tried to fight, while Frederick Wilson, with a cruelly smiling patience, followed him, measured him, and then flattened him with a very accurate one-two that bumped the head of Blackie soundly on the canvas. Friends carried him away, while the crowd groaned loudly. Only a few applauded with vigor. Big John Miller, standing up from his chair on the special dais, with his silver hair blowing and shining, clapped his hands furiously; but Lou Miller merely smiled and waved, and then turned her head. That sort of fighting was not to her taste, it appeared.

Frederick Wilson, in the meantime, had discovered that the fight did not please the crowd, so he stood at the ropes and lifted a gloved hand for silence. When the quiet came, he called in a good, ringing bass voice: 'My friends, I'm sorry that was over so soon. If anybody else will step up, I'll try to please you more the next time.'

Some wit sang out, 'Paging Jack Dempsey!' and the crowd roared.

Then Mortimer found himself getting to his feet.

Lefty Parkman tried to pull him back. 'You're

crazy,' groaned Lefty. 'He's got twenty pounds on you. You can fight, but he can *box*. He'll spear you like a salmon. He'll hold you off and murder you!'

But Mortimer gained his full height and waved to attract attention. He felt as naked as a bad dream, but a bell had struck in his mind that told him his chance had come to lay his hands on the entire range. They despised him for his bookishness. If they could respect him for his manhood the whole story might change. Their hostility was breaking out in the cries with which he was recognized. 'It's the doctor! – It's the dirt doctor!' they shouted. 'Eat him up, tenderfoot! Give him the dirt he wants, Wilson!'

'I'll try to help you entertain,' called Mortimer to Wilson, and hurried back to the dressing tent near the dance floor. He had a glimpse, on the way, of the puzzled face of Lou Miller and of John Miller fairly expanding with expectant pleasure. In the tent he rigged himself in togs that fitted well enough. Blackie sat slumped in a chair at one side, gradually recovering, his eyes still empty and a red drool running from a corner of his mouth.

'How'd it go, Blackie?' asked Parkman.

'I was doin' fine,' said Blackie. 'And then a barn door slammed on my face.'

Lefty Parkman took his champion down through the crowd, and poured savage advice at him every step of the way. 'Keep your left hand

35

up,' he cautioned. 'Don't mind if he raises some bumps with his left. It's his right that rings all the bells. Don't give him a clean shot with it. Keep jabbing. Work in close, and hammer the body. And if you get a chance try the old one-two. Keep the one-two in your head like a song.... And God help you, Chief!'

The strained, anxious faces of the CCC men were the last pictures that Mortimer saw as he squared off with Wilson after the bell. Then a beautiful straight left flashed in his eyes. He ducked under it and dug both hands into the soft of Wilson's body. At least, it should have been the soft, but it was like punching rolls of India rubber.

They came out of the clinch with the crowd suddenly roaring applause for the dirt doctor, but Mortimer knew he had not hurt the big fellow. He had stomach muscles like a double row of clenched fists. And he was smiling as he came in again behind the beautiful, reaching straight left. Mortimer remembered, with a sudden relief, that the rounds were only two minutes long. But merely to endure was not enough. He wanted to wipe Frederick Wilson out of the Miller mind.

He side-stepped the straight left and used his own. It landed neatly, but high on the face. As Wilson shifted in, Mortimer nailed him with the one-two in which Lefty Parkman had drilled him so hard during those remorseless Sundays at the ranch. It stopped Wilson like a wall, but the right

36

hand had not found the button. Mortimer jumped in with a long, straight left to follow his advantage, and the wave of uproar behind him washed him forward. For there is an invincible sympathy with the underdog, in the West, and even the dirt doctor got their cheers as he plunged at big Wilson.

What happened then, Mortimer could not exactly tell. He felt his left miss and slither over the shoulder of Wilson. Then a stick of dynamite exploded in his brain.

He had hurt his knees. That was the next thing he knew. And his brain cleared to admit a tremendous noise of shouting people. He was on hands and knees on the floor of the ring, with the referee swaying an arm up and down beside his face, counting: 'five ... six ... seven ...'

Mortimer came to his feet. He saw Wilson stepping toward him like a giant crane, and the ready left hand was like the crane's beak aimed at a frog. He ducked under the two-handed attack. But the glancing weight of it carried him like a tide of water against the ropes. Head and body, alternately, the punches hammered him. He saw the tight-lipped smile of pleasure and effort as Wilson worked. The man loved his job; and a bursting rage gave Mortimer strength to fight out into the open.

His head was fairly clear, now. He gave as good as he was taking. He noticed that the gloves were

37

soft and big. They might raise lumps, but only a flush hit was apt to break the skin. He threw another long left. And again he felt his arm glance harmlessly over the shoulder of Wilson. Again a blow struck him from nowhere and exploded a bomb of darkness in his brain. Something rapped sharply against the back of his head.

That was the canvas of the ring. He had been knocked flat.

He seemed to be swimming out of a river of blackness with a current that shot him downstream towards disaster. Fiercely he struggled ... and found himself turning on one side, while the swaying arm of the referee seemed to sound the seconds as upon a gong: 'six ... seven ... eight ...'

He got to his knees and saw through a dun-colored fog John Miller waving his arms in exultation; but Lou Miller's face was turned away.

That was why Mortimer got to his feet as the tenth count began. He ducked under the big arms of Wilson and held on. Then the bell rang the end of that round, and the savagely gripping hands of Lefty Parkman were dragging him to his corner.

The whole group of his eight men were piled around him, Erickson weeping with rage, while he and Pudge Major and Dink Waller swung towels to raise a breeze; Chip Ellis and George Masters were massaging his legs, while Bud McGee rubbed the loose of his stomach muscles to restore their normal tension, and Baldy Inman held the

38

water bottle. But Lefty Parkman, clutching him with one arm, whispered or groaned instructions at his ear.

'Lefty, what's he hitting me with?' begged Mortimer.

'Listen, dummy!' said Parkman. 'When you try the straight left he doesn't try to block it. He lets it come and sidesteps. He lets it go over his shoulder, and then he comes in with a right uppercut and nails you.... You got no chance! He's killing you. Lemme say that you've broken your arm! He'll kill you, Chief; and if he does Jan Erickson is going to murder him, and there'll be hell all over the lot! ... Lemme throw in the towel, and you can quit and ...'

'If you throw in the towel ...' said Mortimer through his teeth − but then the gong sounded and he stepped out, feeling as though he were wading against a stiff current of water.

Wilson came right in at him, fiddling with a confident left to make way for a right-hander that would finish the bout; and as the ears of Mortimer cleared he could hear the crowd stamping and shouting, 'Sock him, Doc! ... Break a hole in him! ... Plow him up! ... Hi, Doctor Dirt!'

Wilson dismissed this cheering for the underdog with a twitching grin and lowered his right to invite a left lead.

The wisdom of Lefty Parkman's observations remained in the brain of Mortimer as he saw the opening. It was only a long feint that he used. Instantly the device which Parkman had explained was apparent. Without attempting to block the punch, Wilson side-stepped to slip the blow and, dropping his right, stepped in for á lifting uppercut, his eyes pinched to a glint of white as he concentrated on the knockout wallop.

That was what Mortimer had hoped. The feint he held for an instant until his body almost swayed forward off balance. Then he used the one-two which Lefty had made him master. The right went to the chin no harder, say, than the tapping hammer of the master blacksmith. It gave the distance, the direction for the sledgehammer stroke of the left that followed, and through the soft, thick padding of the glove Mortimer felt his knuckles lodge against the bone of the jaw. He had hit with his full power and Wilson had stepped straight into the blow.

It buckled Wilson's knees. He covered up, instinctively, lurching forward to clinch, and over his shoulder Mortimer saw John Miller with his hands dangling limply, unable to applaud this startling change of fortune. But Lou Miller was on her feet, bent forward.

He saw this double picture. Then he lifted two blows to Wilson's head and sent him swaying back on his heels. There was the whole length of the body open to the next blow, and strained taut, as though a hand had stretched a throat for the butcher's knife. Mortimer plunged his right straight into that defenseless target and doubled it up like a jackknife.

He stepped back as Wilson fell on his knees, embracing his tormented body with one arm. The other hand gestured to the referee.

'Foul!' said the lips of Wilson.

'Get up and fight,' ordered the referee, as he began his count. He was a tough fellow, this referee. He had done some fighting in his youth in Chicago and eastward. Now some of an unforgotten vocabulary flowed from his lips. First, with a wide gesture, he invited the scorn of the crowd and got a howling rejoinder. Then, as he counted, he dropped rare words between the numbers, as: '...three, you yellow skunk ... four, for a four-flusher ... five, a coyote is St. Patrick beside you ... six, for a ring-tailed rat ...'

Wilson struggled to one knee, making faces that indicated dreadful agony; and Mortimer saw John Miller shake both fists in the air and then turn his back in disgust. The interest of Mortimer in the fight ended at that moment. He hardly cared when the referee counted out Wilson the next moment. But, as he climbed through the ropes, the hands of his eight men reached up to clutch him with dangerous hands of congratulation.

Afterward, Lefty Parkman rejoiced in the dressing tent. 'You got it just the way I wanted,' he said. 'You plastered the sucker just as he

41

stepped in. Oh, baby, if you chuck this ranching, I'll make a light heavyweight champ out of you inside three years. Nothing but bacon three times a day, and eggs all day Sunday! ... Say, Chief, will you throw in with me and make a try at it?'

Mortimer smiled vaguely at him. He had something of far greater importance to think about than a ring career, for, as he remembered the enthusiastic voices that had applauded him as he left the ring, it seemed to him that he might have broken through the solid hedge of hostility which had hemmed him in for two years on the range. There remained one great step to take. If he could win over the girl, it would be the greatest evening of his life, and he had determined to play his cards like a crooked gambler if that were necessary to his winning.

'Start drifting around,' he told Lefty. 'Circulate a little and find out how John Miller took the fading of big Wilson. I'll see you later at the barbecue.'

In his anxiety about further consequences he hardly knew what food he tasted when he found a place at one of the long tables in the barbecue glade, but he was keenly aware of favorable and critical eyes which kept studying him, and it was plain that while he had won over a large number of the hostile, his work was not nearly ended. Then Lefty Parkman leaned at his shoulder and murmured, 'Miller is sour. He must have had a whole roll on that Wilson. When you dropped Wilson, Miller said he wished you'd never showed your face on the range.'

That was serious enough; the grave face with which Lou Miller passed him a little later was even more to the point. She was drifting about among the tables to see that everyone had his choice, and when she passed Mortimer all recognition was dead in her eye. But when he turned his head to look after her, she made a slight gesture toward the trees. He waited only a moment before he left the table and went after her. Her pale figure led him through swaying lantern light that set the tree trunks wavering, and on through silver drippings of moonlight until she reached the edge of the woods.

When he came up, she said quietly, 'You must leave at once. Some of the men here hate you, Harry. And my father won't believe that you beat Fred Wilson fairly. He thinks there must have been a foul blow, as Fred claims.'

The hope of winning over John Miller vanished completely. But there remained the girl, and if she were to be placed in immediate charge of the ranch she would be gain enough.

'I can't leave,' he said.

She came closer to him and laid a hand on his arm. The moonlight that slid through a gap in the leaves overhead made silver of her hair, her throat, and her hand. 'You don't understand me,'

43

she said. 'When I say that you ought to go now, I mean that there's really danger for you here.'

'Is your father going to do me in?' he asked.

'He knows nothing about it,' she answered, 'but I know there are a hundred men here who feel sure Father would be glad if you were run off the range. You have to go – now. I'll stay with you until you're off the place.'

He was silent.

'Will you listen to me?' she repeated. 'Harry, I know what you want. You want to open up the entire range to the new ideas. Maybe you're right about them, but none of us can believe it. Do what a wise man ought to do. Give up. Sell out. Try your luck in some other place where your brains will tell. You've poured in two years on this range. You can waste twenty more and never get forward.'

'That's good man-talk,' he said. 'But Lou, do you ever talk like a woman?'

She laughed a little and stepped back from him. 'Well, what's to come now?' she asked.

'Some silly sentimentality,' said Mortimer.

'Between you and me?' she asked, still laughing.

He drew a slow, deep breath, for he had made up his mind that she was no more than a unit of the enemy to be beaten down or won over, as he could, but there seemed in her now such a free courage and frankness, and the moon touched her beauty with such a reverent hand that his heart was touched and he despised the thing he was

44

about to attempt. That weakness lasted only a moment. He went on along the way which he had laid out for himself.

He said, 'Has it ever seemed a little strange to you that I've given up two years of my life to soil conservation in a country where I'm damned before I start, and where I have to share profits and work under the thumb of a drunk like Charlie Hancock?'

'That doesn't sound like sentimentality,' answered the girl. 'It sounds the truth. No, I've never been able to understand you. I've thought you were a sort of metal monster.'

'But you've noticed me carrying on? And till recently you've seen me hounding your father to get his support?'

'Of course I've noticed,' she said.

'Well, can you think of anything except plain foolishness that would keep me at the work here?' he demanded.

'I'm trying to think,' she answered.

'I'll help you,' he said. 'Remember two years ago? You were out here from school. Easter vacation. I was standing in front of the Hancock place. You rode Hampton – zip over the edge of the hill and down the hollow, and then zooming away out of sight beside the ruins of the old windmills. And wings got hold of my heart and lifted me after you.'

He took another breath after the lie. The girl

was still as stone. The moonlight seemed to have frozen her and the airy lightness of her dress. She said nothing.

'What about the announcement of that engagement?' he asked harshly.

'There won't be any announcement. It's ended,' she replied. 'Harry, what are you trying to tell me? You've hardly looked twice at me in two years.'

'I was being the romantic jackass,' he said. 'The stranger with the great vision and the strong hands. I was going to change the whole range, and then offer you my work in one hand and my heart in the other, like some of the driveling fools in the old books.... I *have* been a fool, Lou, but don't laugh at me if you can help it.'

'I won't laugh,' she said.

He went on: 'I thought that if I ruled out everything but the work, I'd get my reward. Instead of that I have the people laughing at me. And I suppose I dreamed that you were receiving radio messages, so to speak, from the fool across the valley who loved you.'

'Love? Love?' said the girl.

'Before I get out of the country like a beaten dog, I had to tell you the truth,' he lied. And yet as he looked at her he wondered if the lie were altogether perfect. 'I don't expect you to do anything except laugh in my face.'

A thudding of hoofbeats and a creaking of

leather came through the trees behind them. She made a gesture, not to him, but to the ground, the world, the air around them.

'I can't laugh,' she said. 'I believe it all.... My heart's going crazy, and I'm dizzy. It's the moonlight, isn't it? It's the crazy moonlight. You're not snapping your fingers and making me fall in love like this, are you?'

From the trees the riders came out softly, the hoofbeats deadened by the leaf mold. There were a thronging dozen of them, with sombreros pulled low and bandannas drawn up and over their mouths to make efficient masks.

One of them sang out, 'Stand back from him, you!' And as the girl sprang away, startled, something whistled in the air over Mortimer's head. The snaky shadow of the rope dropped across his vision, and then he was grappled by the noose, which cunningly pinned his arms against his sides.

TWO

Sam Pearson, the foreman of the huge Miller ranch, was on the saddle end of the rope with a hundred and ninety pounds of seasoned muscle and nearly forty years of range wisdom. He did not have direct orders from Miller, but the indirect suggestions were more than enough for Pearson. He felt, personally, that it was an affront to the entire Miller legend to have this hostile interloper on the ranch at the barbecue; and there was a virtuous thrill in his hand as he settled that noose around Mortimer's arms.

Sam's mount, which was his best cutting horse, spun like a top and took Mortimer in tow at a mild canter over the flat and then down the slope of the Chappany valley. The screaming protests of Lou Miller shrilled and died out far to the rear, quite drowned by the uproar of Pearson's cowpunchers. They all had plenty of liquor under their belts;

they all felt they were striking a good stroke for the best cause in the world; and the result was that their high spirits unleashed like a pack of wolves. Like wolves they howled as they dashed back and forth around Pearson and his captive. And, as their delight grew, more than one quirt snapped in an expert hand to warm the seat of Mortimer's pants.

The Easterner ran well, Pearson had to admit; he kept up a good sprint, which prevented him from falling on his face and being dragged, until they came over the edge of the level and dropped onto the slant ground, with the five Chappany lakes glimmering silver-bright in the hollow beneath them.

At that point Pearson's rope went slack, and he saw Mortimer spin head over heels like a huge ball of tumbleweed. It was so deliciously funny to Sam Pearson that he reeled in the saddle with hearty laughter. He was still howling with joy and the shrill cowboy yells were sticking needles in his ears when a very odd thing happened, for the whirling, topsy-turvy body of Mortimer regained footing and balance for an instant, while running with legs made doubly long by the pitch of the slope, and, like a great black, deformed cat he flung himself onto Monte McLean, who rode close to his side.

There was plenty of silver-clear moonlight to show Monte defending himself from that savage and unexpected attack. Monte was a good, two-handed fighter and he whanged the Easterner over the head and shoulders, not with the lash, but with the loaded butt of his quirt. However, in an instant Mortimer had swarmed up the side of the horse and wrapped Monte in his arms.

This was highly embarrassing to Pearson. If he yanked Mortimer off that mustang, he would bring Monte down to the ground with him. If he did not yank Mortimer out of the saddle, the Easterner would probably throttle Monte and get away. There was another thing that caused Pearson to groan and that was the realization that he had kept the tenderfoot on such a loose rope that he had been able to work his arms and hands up through the biting grip of the noose. He was held now like an organ-grinder's monkey, around the small of the waist.

Other trouble came on the run toward Sam Pearson. A cry came ringing to him, and he saw a girl on a horse stretched in a dead gallop come tilting over the upper edge of the slope. That would be Lou Miller. She was a good girl and as Western as they come. But there is a sharp limit to the feminine sense of humor, and it was as likely as not that the girl thought this was a lynching party instead of a mere bit of Western justice and range discipline. The idea was, in brief, to start Mortimer running toward the horizon and encourage him to keep on until he was out of sight.

Sam Pearson simply did not know what to do, and therefore he did the most instinctive thing, which was to give a good tug on the rope. To his horror, he saw both Monte and Mortimer slew sidewise from the saddle and spill to the ground.

They kept on rolling for a dozen yards, and then they lay still, one stretched beside the other. Big Sam Pearson got his horse to the place and dived for the spot where Monte lay. He picked the fallen cowpuncher up. The loose of the body spilled across his arm as he shouted, 'Monte! Hey, Monte! A little spill like that didn't do nothing to you, did it? Hey, Monte, can't you hear me?'

The other cowpunchers came piling up on their horses, bringing a fog-white rolling of dust that poured over Monte. And he, presently rousing with a groan, brought a cheer from them. They set him up on his feet and felt him from head to foot for broken bones. They patted his back to start him breathing.

'Put him into a saddle,' said Sam Pearson. 'Old Monte'll be himself when he feels the stirrups under his feet.'

So they put Monte into a saddle and steadied him there with many hands. In fact, he reached out at once with a vaguely fumbling hand for the reins and then mumbled, 'He kind of got hold of me like a wildcat, and he wouldn't loosen up.'

Here the wild voice of Louise Miller cried close by, 'Sam Pearson! You murderer, Sam, you've killed him! You've killed him!'

The foreman, still with a hand on Monte, turned and saw the girl on her knees beside the prostrate body of Mortimer. But at that moment the Easterner groaned heavily, and sat up. And Pearson took that as a signal to go.

'Let's get out of here on the jump, boys,' he said. 'Maybe we scratched up more hell'n we reckoned on.'

He hit the saddle as he spoke, and in the center of the cavalcade struck out at a gallop for the ranch house, with the wavering figure of Monte held erect by two friendly riders. For Pearson wanted to get in his report of strange happenings to an employer who had never yet been hard on him....

Mortimer, sitting up with his head bowed by shock and the nausea of deep pain and bruises, saw the world very dimly for a moment. Next he felt an increasing sharp pain from a rent in his scalp near the crown of the head, where the braided handle of Monte's quirt had glanced in striking; and finally he was aware of a warm, small trickle of blood that ran down the side of his face and dripped off his chin.

'Come back! Sam! Sam! Come back!' shouted a girl's voice. Then two hands took him by the cheeks and tilted back his head. 'They've killed

53

him!' whispered Lou Miller. 'The cowards! The cowards! They've killed Harry Mortimer!'

He could not see her very clearly because the dazzle of the moon was above her head, and to his bleared eyes her face was a darkness of almost featureless shadow. But the moon flowed like water over one bare shoulder, where the chiffon had been torn away, during her headlong riding. These pictures he saw clearly enough, though he could not put them together and make connected sense of them.

As for what had happened immediately before, he could not make head nor tail of it, and it seemed to him that he was still telling the girl that he loved her now, even now, though his brain reeled and the nausea kept his stomach working.

That was why he said, 'If I were dying, I'd want to say a last thing to you, Lou.... I love you.'

'Harry, are you dying? Are you dying, darling?' cried the girl.

She took the weight of his head and shoulders across her lap and in her arms. There was still dust in the air, but there was a smell of sweet, soapy cleanness about her.

'I'm all right,' he told her. Then the theme recurred to him, and he drove himself on to the words: 'I love you.... D'you laugh at me when I tell you that? ... I love you!'

'And I love you, Harry.... D'you hear? Can you understand?' she answered.

The words registered one by one in his mind but they had no connected meaning. They were like a useless hand in poker.

'Tell me where you're hurt,' said the girl. 'Tell me where the worst pain is, Harry.'

He closed his eyes. He felt that he had lost in his great effort. He was not finished. He would still try to make her love him, because, beyond her, opened the gates of a new future which he could bring to the range; beyond her lay unending miles of the pleasant grasslands and the futures of ten thousand happy men. He felt that he was like a general who needed to carry by assault only one small redoubt and then the great fight would be won.

That assault would have to be made in the future. Now, with closed eyes, he could only mutter, 'You smell like a clean bath … you smell like a clean wind.'

She slipped from beneath his weight. He heard cloth suddenly torn into strips. The sound went through his brain and found sore places and tortured them. Then the blood was being wiped from his face and the long bandage was wound about his head, firmly. But it gave no pain. Wherever she touched him the pain disappeared. Then she had his head and shoulders in her lap again, and one hand supported his head.

'Wherever you touch me – it's queer – the pain goes,' said Mortimer.

'Because I love you!' said the girl.

55

He regarded the words with a blank stare and found no meaning in them. 'Are you laughing at me?' he said.

'I'm only loving you,' said the girl. 'Don't speak. Lie still. Only tell where the pain is.'

'God put a gift in your hands. They take the pain away,' said Mortimer. 'What color are your eyes?'

'Kind of a gray, blue-green.... I don't know what color they are,' she said. 'Don't talk, Harry. Lie still.'

One instant of clarity came to him. He got to his feet with a sudden, immense effort and stood swaying. 'My men are back there in trouble!' he groaned. 'Leave me here. Go back and stop the fight if you can. I'll come along on foot and help out.'

'There'll be no more trouble. That Sam Pearson, like a coward, has made trouble enough for one night. He won't lift his hand again. But can you get into the saddle? I'll help ... get into the saddle ... lift your left foot.'

He had his grip on the horn of the saddle and stood for a time with his head dropped against the sharp cantle, while the whirling, nauseating darkness spun through his brain. The orders came to him again, insistently. He raised his left foot. A hand guided it into the stirrup.

'Now one big heave, and you'll be in the saddle. Come on, and up you go.'

56

He felt an ineffectual force tugging and lifting at him; his muscles automatically responded and he found himself slumped in the saddle, his head hanging far down. There was no strength in the back of his neck. He wanted to vomit. But there was that uncompleted battle which had to be fought.

'Are you gone?' said Mortimer. 'I love you!'

Then a blowing darkness overcame his brain again. He managed to keep his hands locked on the pommel; and the nausea covered his body with cold runnels of sweat. A voice entered his mind from far ahead, sometimes speaking clearly, and sometimes as dim and far as though it were blowing away on a wind. Whenever he heard it, new strength came into him, and hope with it.

It told him to endure. It said that they had reached the bridge. In fact, he heard the hoofbeats of the horse strike hollow beneath him. He saw, dimly, the silver of water under the moon. The voice said they were nearing the Hancock place, if only he could hold on a little. But he knew that he could not hold on. A sense like that of sure prophecy told him that he was about to die and that he never would reach the haven of the ranch house.

And then, suddenly, the outlines of the house were before him.

He steeled himself to endure the dismounting, to gather strength that would pull his leg over the back of the horse.

Now he was standing beside it, wavering.

He made a vast effort to steer his feet toward the faintly lighted doorway. The girl tried to support him and guide him. Then many heavy footfalls rushed out about him. The voice of Jan Erickson roared out like the furious, huge, wordless bellowing of a bull. The enormous hands and arms of Jan Erickson lifted him, cradled him lightly, took him through the doorway.

'Louise,' he whispered, 'I love you ...'

He could make out the sound of her voice, but not the answering words. Clearer to his mind was the sense of wonderful relief in finding his men back safely, at the Hancock place. He wanted to give thanks for that. He felt stinging tears of gratitude under his eyelids and kept his eyes closed, so that the tears should not be seen.

He could hear Lefty Parkman screech out like a fighting tomcat, 'Look at his face! ... Look at his *face!* Oh, God, look what they've done to him! Look what they gone and done to the chief!'

And there was Pudge Major giving utterance in a strange, weeping whine: 'They dragged him. They took and dragged him. They took and dragged him like a stinking coyote.'

'Get out of my way!' shouted Jan Erickson. 'I'm gunna kill some of 'em!'

The stairs creaked. They were taking him up to his room. The air was much hotter inside the

58

house, and warmer and warmer the higher they carried him. But he began to relax toward sleep.

The girl, running up the stairs behind the men, cried out to them that she wanted to help tend him. One of the brown-faced, big-shouldered fellows turned and looked at her as no man had ever looked at her before.

'Your dirty, sneaking crowd done this to the chief!' he said. 'Why don't you go back where you come from? Why don't you go and crow and laugh about it, like the others are doing? Go back and tell your pa that we're gunna have blood for this. We're gunna wring it out, like water out of the Monday wash! ... Get out!'

Lefty Parkman left the house and sprinted away for a car to drive to Poplar Springs for a doctor; and Louise Miller went down the stairs into the hall.

The angry, muttering voices of the CCC men passed on out of her ken, and the blond giant who was carrying the weight of Mortimer so lightly. She looked helplessly into the parlor, and there saw Charles Hancock lying on his couch dressed in shorts and a jacket of thin Chinese silk, with the materials for his rum punch scattered over the table beside him. He got up when he saw her and waved his hand. He seemed made of differing component parts – prematurely old boy, and decayed scholar, and drunken satirist.

'Come in, Lou,' he said. 'Your boys been having

59

a little time for themselves beating up Harry Mortimer? ... Come in and have a drink of this punch. You look as though you need it. You look as though you'd been through quite a stampede yourself!'

She became aware for the first time of the torn chiffon and her bare shoulder. The bleared, sneering eyes of Charlie Hancock made her feel naked. But she had to have an excuse for staying in the house until she had a doctor's opinion about Mortimer's condition. The picture of the dragging, tumbling body at the end of the rope kept running like a madness through her memory, and the closing eyes and the battered lips that said he loved her. For love like that, which a man commingles with his dying breath, it seemed to the girl, was a sacred thing which most people never know; and the glory of it possessed her strongly, like wings lifting her heart. Such a knowledge was given to her, she thought, that she had become mature. The girl of that afternoon was a child and a stranger to her in thought and in feeling.

She was so filled with unspeakable tenderness that even that rum-bloated caricature of a man, Charles Hancock, was a figure she could look upon with a gentle sympathy. For he, after all, had been living in the same house with the presence of Harry Mortimer for two long years. Viewed in that light, he became a treasure house from which, perhaps, she could draw a thousand priceless reminiscences about the man she loved. That was why she went to Hancock with a smile and shook his moist, fat hand warmly.

'I will have a drink,' she said. 'I need one.'

'Wang!' shouted Hancock. 'Hot water.... Take this chair, Lou.... And don't look at the rug and the places where the wallpaper is peeling. Our friend Mortimer says that this is a pigpen. He won't live here with me. That connoisseur of superior living prefers to spend most of his time with the gang of brutes in the big shed behind the houses. Sings with 'em; sings for 'em; dances for 'em; does a silly buck and wing just to make 'em laugh; plays cards with 'em; gives up his life to 'em the way a cook serves his steak on a platter.... By the way, did your boys break any of the Mortimer bones?'

His eyes waited with a cruelly cold expectancy. Loathing went into a shudder through the marrow of her bones, but she kept herself smiling, wondering how Mortimer had endured two years of this. She thought of the years of her own life as a vain blowing hither and thither, but at last she had come to a stopping point. Her heart poured out of her toward the injured man who lay above them, where the heavy footfalls trampled back and forth and deep-throated, angry murmuring continued.

'I don't know how badly he's injured,' she said. 'I don't think any bones ... if there isn't internal

61

injury ... but God wouldn't let him be seriously hurt by brutes and cowards!'

Hancock looked at her with a glimmering interest rising in his eyes. 'Ah, ha!' he chuckled. 'I see.✗

She had her drink, by that time, and she paused in the careful sipping of it. 'You see what, Charlie?' she asked.

He laughed outright, this time. 'I put my money against it. I wouldn't have believed it,' he said.

'What wouldn't you have believed?' asked the girl.

'For my part,' said Hancock, 'I love living, Lou. I love to let the years go by like a stream, because ... do you know why?'

'I don't know,' she answered, watching him anxiously and wondering if he were very drunk.

He took a swallow that emptied his glass, and with automatic hands began brewing another potion. Still his shoulders shook with subdued mirth.

'I don't want to be rude, but ...' said Hancock, and broke into a peal of new laughter.

The girl flushed. 'I can't understand you at all, Charlie,' she said.

'Can't understand me? Tut, tut! I'm one of the simple ones. I'm understood at a glance. I'm clear glass ... I'm not one of the cloudy, mysterious figures like Mortimer.'

'Why is he cloudy and mysterious?' she asked.

'To go in one direction for two years, and wind up on the opposite side of the horizon ... that's a mystery, isn't it?' asked Hancock, with his bursting chuckle.

'Two years in one direction?' she repeated, guessing, and then blushing, and hating herself for the color which, she knew, was pouring up across her face.

Hancock watched her with a surgeon's eye. He shook his head as he murmured, 'I wouldn't believe it. All in a tremor ... and blushing. Mystery? Why, the man's loaded with mystery!'

'Charlie,' she said, 'if I know what you're talking about, I don't like it very well.'

'Oh, we'll change the subject, then, of course,' said Hancock. 'Only thing in the world I'm trained to do is to try to please the ladies. You never guessed that, Lou, did you? You see, I don't succeed very well, but I keep on trying.'

'Trying to please us?' she asked.

'Yes, trying. But I never really succeed. Not like the men of mystery. They don't waste time on gestures. They simply step out – and they bring home the bacon!'

He laughed again, rubbing his hands.

'Are you talking about Harry Mortimer and me?' she asked, taking a deep breath as she forced herself to come to the point.

'Talking about nothing to offend you,' said Hancock. 'Wouldn't do it for the world.... Can't tell you how I admire that Mortimer. Shall I tell you why?'

She melted at once. 'Yes, I want to hear it,' she said.

'Ah, there you are with the shining eyes and the parted lips,' said Hancock. 'And that's the picture he said he would paint, too. And here it is, painted!'

The words lifted her slowly from her chair.

Hancock was laughing too heartily to be aware of her. 'Mystery? He's the deepest man of mystery I've ever known in my life,' he said. 'There's the end of the road for him. No way to get ahead. Blocked on every side in his mission of teaching us all how to use the range and button the grass to the ground permanently. He's blocked; can't get past John Miller.... But if he can't get past John Miller, at least he can get past an easier obstacle. And he does!'

He laughed again, still saying, through his laughter, 'But the rich Lou Miller, the beautiful Lou Miller, the spark of fire, the whistle in the wind, the picture that shines in every man's eyes ...' Here laughter drowned his voice.

'Sit down, Lou!' he said. 'I tell you, I love an efficient man, and that's why I love this Mortimer. If he can't win the men, he'll try the women. Two years in one direction gets him nothing. So he turns around and goes in the opposite direction, and all at once he's home! Wonderful, I call it.

64

Simply wonderful! And in a single evening! Even if he's beaten up a bit, he comes safely home and brings Beauty beside the Beast. Knew he would, too. Ready to bet on it.'

'To bet on it?' asked the girl, feeling a coldness of face as though a strong wind were blowing against her.

'What did I say?' asked Hancock.

'Nothing,' said the girl.

'Sit down, Lou.'

'No, I have to go home. The barbecue is still running. Hundreds of people there.... Good-by, Charlie!'

'Oh, but you can't go like this. I have a thousand things to tell you about Mortimer.'

'I think I've heard enough,' said the girl. 'I didn't realize that he was such a man of – of mystery. But you're right, Charlie. I suppose you're right.'

She felt the bitter emotion suddenly swelling and choking in her throat, for she was remembering how Mortimer, stunned and mindless after his fall, had clung still to a monotonous refrain, telling her over and over again that he loved her. She knew that he was a fighting man, and he had clung like a bulldog to his appointed task of winning her even when the brain was stunned. The clearest picture before her mind was of the two men talking in this room, with laughter shaking the paunch of Charlie Hancock as he bet with Mortimer that the tenderfoot could not go to

65

the barbecue and put Lou Miller in his pocket. Shame struck her with the edge and coldness of steel. She turned suddenly and went out into the moonlight to where Hampton was waiting....

When Mortimer wakened late that night he heard the snoring of three of the Hancock cowpunchers in an adjoining room. His brain was perfectly clear now, and only when he moved in his bed did he feel the soreness of bruised muscles.

'How you coming, Chief?' asked the voice of Jan Erickson.

He looked up into the face of the huge Swede, who was leaning from his chair, a shadow wrapped in bright moonlight.

'I'm fit and fine,' said Mortimer. 'Go to bed, Jan.'

'I ain't sleepy,' declared Jan Erickson. 'Tell me who done it to you.'

'A few drunken cowpunchers,' said Mortimer.

'Was that big feller Wilson one of them? The feller you licked?'

'No. He wasn't one of them.'

'That's good,' said Erickson, 'because he's taken and run away from the Chappany. He didn't like the side of the range that you showed him, and he run off to Poplar Springs on his way back home. But what was the names of the others?'

'I didn't recognize them,' lied Mortimer.

'It was some of Miller's men, wasn't it?' persisted Jan.

'I don't think so,' answered Mortimer. 'Stop bothering me and go to bed, Jan.'

'How many was there?' asked Erickson, a whine of eagerness in his voice.

'A crowd. I couldn't recognize anyone. It's all over. Forget it.'

Erickson was silent for a moment, and then his whisper reached Mortimer: 'God strike me if I forget it!' ...

A healthy man can sleep off most of his physical troubles. Mortimer was not roused in the morning when the Hancock cowpunchers clumped down the stairs with jingling spurs. He slept on till almost noon, and then wakened from a melancholy dream to find the wind whistling and moaning around the house and the temperature fallen far enough to put a shiver in his body. When he stood up there were only a few stiffnesses in his muscles. The night before, it was apparent, he simply had been punch-drunk.

A bucket of water in a galvanized iron washtub made him a bath. As he sloshed the chill water over his body his memory stepped back into the dimness of the previous evening. Most of it was a whirling murk through which he could remember the nodding head of Hampton, bearing him forward, and the perpetual disgust of nausea, and his own voice saying, 'I love you!' That memory struck him into a sweat of anxious shame until the foggy veil lifted still farther. He could not

67

remember her answer in words, but he could recall the tenderness of her voice and how her arms had held him.

Lightning jagged before Mortimer's eyes and split open his old world to the core. First a sense of guilt ran with his pulses, like the shadowy hand of the referee counting out the seconds of the knockdown. But she never would know, he told himself, if a life of devotion could keep her from the knowledge. He had gone to her ready to lie like a scoundrel, and he had come away with the thought of her filling his mind like a light. Slowly toweling his body dry, he fell into a muse, re-seeing her, body and spirit. That high-headed pride now seemed to him no more than the jaunty soul which is born of the free range. That fierce loyalty which kept her true to her father in every act and word would keep her true to a husband in the same way. She never could turn again, he told himself. And he saw his life extending like a smooth highway to the verge of the horizon. With her hand to open the door to him and give him authority, he would have the entire range, very soon, using those methods which would give the grasslands eternal life. He had been almost hating the stupid prejudices and the blindness of the ranchers; now his heart opened with understanding of them all.

He dressed with stumbling hands, and noted the purple bruised places and where the skin had rubbed away in spots, but there was nothing worth a child's notice except a dark, swollen place that half covered his right eye and extended back across the temple. He could shrug his shoulders at such injuries, if only the scalp wound were not serious. When he had shaved, he went out to the barracks shed to let Shorty examine the cut.

Shorty took off the bandage, washed the torn scalp, and wound a fresh bandage in place. 'Healing up like nobody's business,' he said. 'Sit down and leave me throw a steak and a coupla handfuls of onions into you, and you'll be as fine as a fiddle again.'

So Mortimer sat down to eat, and was at his second cup of coffee before he remembered the time of day. It was half an hour past noon and yet his CCC gang had not showed up for food.

'Shorty, where the devil are the boys?' he asked. 'What's happened? You're not cooking lunch for them?'

'Well, the fact is that they sashayed off on a kind of a little trip,' said Shorty.

Mortimer stared at him. 'They left the ranch without talking to me?' he demanded.

'They thought you'd be laid up today,' said Shorty. 'And so they kind of went and played hooky on you, Chief.'

'Shorty, where did they go?' asked Mortimer, remembering vividly how Jan Erickson had leaned over his bed during the night and had tried

69

to drag from him the identity of his assailants.

'How would I know where they'd go?' asked Shorty.

Mortimer turned his back on the cook, for he knew that he would get no trustworthy information from him. He tried to think back into the mind of his gang – not into their individual brains but into the mob-consciousness which every group possesses, and the first thing that loomed before him was their savage, deep, unquestioning devotion to him.

With a sick rush of apprehension, he wondered if they might have gone across the valley straight to the Miller place to exact vengeance for the fall of their chief. But Lefty Parkman and Pudge Major were far too levelheaded to permit a move as wild as that. If they wanted to make trouble for men of the Miller ranch they would go to Poplar Springs and try to find straggling groups of the cowpunchers from the big outfit.

Mortimer jumped for the corner of the room and picked up a rifle. He put it down again, straightening slowly. When it came to firearms, his CCC lads were helpless, as compared with the straight-shooting men of the range. He, himself, was only a child in that comparison.

He turned and ran empty-handed into the adjoining shed. The big truck was gone, as he had expected, but the one-ton truck remained, and into the seat of this he climbed in haste.

It was fifteen miles to Poplar Springs and he did the distance in twenty minutes. As he drove he took dim note of the day. The melancholy wind which had wakened him still mourned down the valley, but its force along the ground was nothing compared to the velocity of the upper air. What seemed to be fast-traveling clouds, unraveled and spread thin, shot out of the northwest and flattened the arch of the sky, with the sun sometimes golden, sometimes dull and green, through that unusual mist. In the west the mountains had disappeared.

Three from north to south, three from east to west, the streets of Poplar Springs laid out a small checkering of precise little city blocks. Most of its life came from the 'springs,' whose muddy waters were said to have some sort of medicinal value. An old frame hotel spread its shambling wings around the water. A rising part of the town's business, however, came from the aviation company of Chatham, Armstrong & Worth, which had built some hangars and used the huge flat east of the place as a testing ground. Saturday nights were the bright moments for Poplar Springs, when the cowpunchers rode into town or drove rattling automobiles in from the range to patronize the saloons which occupied almost every corner.

Wherever he saw a pedestrian, Mortimer called, 'Seen anything of a six-foot-four Swede with hair as pale as blow-sand?' At last he was directed to Porson's Saloon.

Porson's had been there in Poplar Springs since the earliest cattle days and still used the old swing doors with three bullet holes drilled through the slats of one panel and two through another. If Porson's had filled a notch for each of its dead men, it would have had to crowd fifty-three notches on one gun butt, people said, for bar whisky and old cattle feuds and single-action Colts had drenched its floor with blood more than once. An echo of the reputation of the place was ominous in Mortimer's mind as he pushed through the doors.

It was like stepping into a set piece on a stage. The picture he dreaded to find was there in every detail. Jan Erickson, Pudge Major, Lefty Parkman, George Masters, and Dink Waller stood at the end of the bar nearest the door, and bunched at the farther end were eight of the Miller cowpunchers, with Sam Pearson dominating the group. The bartender was old Rip Porson himself, carrying his seventy years like a bald-headed eagle. Unperturbed by the silent thunder in the air, he calmly went about serving drinks.

Mortimer stood a moment inside the door, with his brain whirling as though he had been struck on the base of the skull. The Miller punchers looked at him with a deadly interest. Not one of his own men turned a head toward him, but Lefty Parkman said in a low voice, 'The chief!'

'Thank God!' muttered Pudge Major. But Dink Waller growled, 'He oughta be home! This is our job.'

'It's time for a round on the house, boys,' said Rip Porson. 'And I wanta tell you something: The first man that goes for iron while he's drinkin' on the house, he gets a slug out of my own gun.... Here's to you, one and all!'

He had put out the bottles of rye and, as the round was filled, silently, he lifted his own glass in a steady red claw.

The two factions continued to stare with fascinated attention at each other, eye holding desperately to eye as though the least shift in concentration would cause disaster. They raised their glasses as Rip Porson proposed his toast: 'Here's to the fight and to them that shoot straight; and damn the man that breaks the mirror.'

In continued silence the men of the Miller place and Mortimer's CCC gang drank.

Then Mortimer walked to the bar. He chose a place directly between the two hostile forces, standing exactly in the field of fire, if guns were once drawn. 'I'll have a beer,' he said.

Rip Porson dropped his hands on the edge of the bar and regarded Mortimer with bright, red-stained eyes. 'You're the one that the trouble's all about, ain't you?' he asked. 'You're Harry Mortimer, ain't you?'

'I am,' said Mortimer. 'And there's going to be no more trouble.'

'Beer is what the man's having,' said Porson, slowly filling a glass. A smile, or the ghost of a smile, glimmered in his old eyes.

'Set them up, Porson,' said the low, deep voice of Jan Erickson.

'Set 'em up over here, too,' commanded Sam Pearson.

The bartender pushed the whisky bottles into place again. Every moment he was growing more cheerful.

Mortimer faced his own men. 'Lefty!' he said, picking out the most dominant spirit from among them.

Lefty Parkman gave not the slightest sign that he had heard the voice which spoke to him. He had picked out a single face among the cowpunchers and was staring at his man with a concentrated hatred. Odds made no difference to Lefty, even odds of eight to six when all the eight were heeled with guns and hardly two of the CCC men could have any weapons better than fists.

'Lefty!' repeated Mortimer.

The eyes of Lefty wavered suddenly toward his chief.

'Turn around and walk out the door. We're getting out of here,' said Mortimer, 'and you're leading the way.'

The glance of Lefty slipped definitely away from

the eye of Mortimer and fixed again on its former target. For the first time an order from Mortimer went disregarded.

Among Sam Pearson's men there was a bowlegged cowpuncher named Danny Shay, barrel-chested, bull-browed, and as solid as the stump of a big tree. The croak of a resonant bullfrog was in the voice of Danny and it was this voice which now said, 'There ain't room enough in here for 'em; we got the air kind of used up, maybe.'

One of the cowpunchers laughed at this weak sally, a brief, half-hysterical outburst of mirth.

Pudge Major lurched from his place at the bar and walked straight toward the Miller men.

'Go back, Pudge!' commanded Mortimer.

Pudge strode on, unheeding. 'You look like an ape when you laugh,' said Pudge. 'When you open your face that wide, I can see the baboon all the way down the red of your dirty throat.'

Mortimer turned and saw Jed Wharton, among the cowpunchers, hit Pudge fairly on the chin with a lifting punch. Major rocked back on his heels and began an involuntary retreat. Big Jed Wharton followed with a driving blow from which Pudge Major cringed away with both hands flung up and a strange little cry of fear that made Mortimer's blood run cold. Poor Major had gone for bigger game than his nature permitted, and the sight of the white feather among his men

75

struck into Mortimer's brain like a hand of shadow.

He saw in the leering, triumphant faces of the cowpunchers the charge that was about to follow. The man next to Sam Pearson was already drawing his Colt. He had no chance to glance behind him at his own followers, but Mortimer could guess that they were as heartsick and daunted as he by the frightened outcry of Pudge. And he remembered the barking voice of an assistant football coach hounding him into scrimmage when he was a freshman at college: 'Low, Mortimer! Tackle low!'

'Tackle low!' yelled Mortimer, and dived at Sam Pearson's knees. While he was still in the air he saw from the corner of his eye Lefty Parkman swarming in to the attack, and the blond head of gigantic Erickson. Then his shoulder banged into Pearson's knees, and the whole world seemed to fall on his back.

It was not the sort of barroom fighting that a Westerner would expect. That headlong plunge and the charge of Erickson jammed the cowpunchers against the wall. Mortimer, in the midst of confusion, caught at stamping feet and struggling legs and pulled down all he could reach.

He put his knee on Pearson's neck and pressed on toward Danny Shay, who had been tripped and had fallen like a great frog, on hands and knees.

There was hardly room for fist work. Mortimer jerked his elbow into the face of Danny and stood up in the room Shay had occupied.

Guns were sounding, by that time. As he straightened in the thundering uproar he saw a contorted face not a yard away and a Colt levelling at him over the shoulder of another man. But an arm and fist like a brass-knuckled walking beam struck from a height, and the gunman disappeared into the heap.

That was Jan Erickson's work.

Other men might dance away from Jan and cut him to gradual bits in the open, but for a close brawl he was peerless, and now his hands were filled with work as they never had been before. As Mortimer struck out, he saw on the far side of the bar old Rip Porson standing regardless of danger from chance bullets, with his eyes half closed as he shook his head in a profound disgust.

Mortimer saw Pudge Major in it, also. As though the first touch of fear had turned into a madness, Pudge Major came in with an endless screech, like a fighting cat. He ran into the clubbed butt of a revolver that knocked him back against the wall. From that wall he rebounded, swinging a chair in his hands. The chair landed with a crash of splintering wood. Big Sam Pearson, who had managed to regain his feet at last, sank under the blow, and suddenly Mortimer saw that the fight was ended. Those whom

Erickson had hit solidly were down, to remain down. Dink Waller patiently, uncomplainingly, was throttling his chosen victim with a full Nelson. Lefty pounded a defenseless victim against the wall. George Masters was in a drunken stagger, trying to come toward the noise of battle; but the fight was ended.

The attack had been so quick and close that most of the guns were not even drawn. Hardly half a dozen bullets had hit ceiling or floor. Not a single shot struck flesh; but the great mirror behind the bar was drilled cleanly through the center and from that hole a hundred cracks jagged outward.

'Take their guns!' shouted Mortimer. 'Let them be, but take their guns! Jan, it's over!'

Some two minutes after Mortimer dived at Pearson's knees he had eight revolvers and several large knives piled on the bar. Two or three of the beaten men were staggering to their feet. Danny Shay nursed his bleeding face in both hands. Sam Pearson sat in a corner with blood streaming down from his gashed head, which hung helplessly over one shoulder, agape with the shock, and agrin with pain.

Jan Erickson, still in a frenzy, strode back and forth, shouting, 'That's what a Mortimer does. He cuts through bums like you the way a knife cuts through cheese.... Why don't he wring your necks? Because he's ashamed to hurt wet-nosed kids like you are!'

'Get out of the place, Jan,' commanded Mortimer. 'All of you get out! There are no broken bones, I think, and thank God for that. Get our men out, Jan!'

He turned back to the bar and said to Porson, 'I'll pay half the cost of that mirror, bartender.'

His voice could not penetrate the hazy trance of Rip Porson, who continued to stare into space and wag his head slowly from side to side, as he repeated, 'Fourteen wearing pants and not one man among 'em ... the world has gone to hell ... fourteen milk-fed baboons!' ...

There had to be a few rounds of drinks to celebrate the victory. There had to be some patching of cuts. So it was two hours before Mortimer rounded up his crew and had them back at the Hancock place, with the three men who had missed the fight in agonies because they had been out of it.

'Shut up your faces,' said Jan Erickson. 'There wouldn't of *been* no fight if you'd all been there. They wouldn't of dared.... But the sweet spot you missed was the chief taking a dive into them like into a swimming pool; and the waves he throwed up took all the fight out of them.'

Pudge Major sat with his head in his hands when they were in the barracks shed. Mortimer, on one knee beside him patted him on the back.

'I was yella,' groaned Pudge. 'I was a dirty rat. The whole world knows that I'm yella.'

79

'You needed a sock on the chin before you got your second wind,' declared Mortimer. 'And then you were the best man in the room. Ask the boys. Even Jan wouldn't take you on. Would you, Jan?'

'Him? I'd rather take on a wildcat!' said Jan.

'Jan, d'you mean that, partly?' asked Pudge.

'I mean the whole of it,' said Jan Erickson. 'And when it comes to working with a chair, you're away out by yourself. You're the class of the field.'

Therefore Mortimer left them in this triumphant humor and drove over to the Miller place in the light truck. A Chinese servant opened the door to him but there was no need for him to enter, for John Miller at that moment came down the hall with a jangle of spurs and a quirt in his hand. His daughter was following him. And now he stood tall in the entrance, looking at Mortimer without a word.

'I dare say that you've heard about the trouble in Poplar Springs,' said Mortimer. 'I want to tell you that I didn't send out my men to make trouble; they went off by themselves, and I started after them to bring them back. When I found them, they'd located your people already. I tried to stop the fight, but it got under way in spite of me.'

'Are you through?' asked John Miller, parting his locked jaws with difficulty.

Mortimer said slowly, 'If any reprisals start, it will be from your part, not mine. I've taken my beating and I haven't yipped. But if your fellows

80

come on to make more trouble there'll be murder all over the range. I want to know if you think you can keep your people in hand.'

'Are you finished?' asked Miller.

'I am,' said Mortimer.

'Very well,' said Miller, and walked straight past him.

He turned his bewildered eyes on the girl, as she seemed about to go past him behind her father. His glance stopped her. She was pale; small lines and shadows made her eyes seem older. He had stopped her with his puzzled look, but now as she stood back with a hand against the wall she was looking steadily into his face.

'I wasn't hard, was I?' she asked. 'You only had to whistle and the bird flew right off the tree to your hand. Nothing could be easier than that, could it?'

'What are you saying, Lou?' he asked.

She looked down at his extended hand and then up to the pain in his face before she laughed a little. 'You *are* wonderful, Harry,' she said. 'It's that honest, straightforward simplicity which gets you so far. And then your voice. That does a lot. And the facial expression, too. It's good enough for a close-up. Ah, but Hollywood could make a star of you.... The way it is now, I suppose you hardly make pocket money out of the girls. Or do they run high, sometimes – the bets you place before you go out to make a girl?'

81

'Hancock ... there was no bet ... Lou ... it was only that I didn't know I'd adore you as I do,' stammered Mortimer.

'You know now, though, don't you?' said the girl. 'You love me all your heart can hold, Harry, don't you?'

He tried to answer her, but felt the words die on his lips.

'And d'you know, Harry,' said the girl, peering at him, 'that I think it was the beginning of a great love? As I went along beside you through the night, I would have given up both hands for you. I would have given my face for you. I would have given my heart. And ... aren't you a rather yellow sort of dog, Harry?'

He saw her go by him with that quick, light, graceful step. Something made him look up as she vanished through the patio gate, and he seemed to find an answer for his question in the swift gray stream that poured across the sky endlessly, as it had been pouring ever since the morning. The sun was small and green behind it.

He got back into the truck and drove blindly toward the ranch. The subconscious mind inside him took note of the gray sweep of mist through the sky and the color of the setting sun behind it. It was not water vapor which could give that color, he knew. It was dust – dust rushing on the higher stratum of the air, headlong. Somewhere the wind had eaten through the skin of the range and was

82

bearing uncounted tons of topsoil into nothingness.

That fact should have meant something to Mortimer, but his conscious mind refused to take heed of it, for it was standing still before the thought of Louise Miller. Then Hancock jumped into his mind and he gripped the wheel so hard that it trembled under his grasp.

He brought the car up short before the entrance of the house. Three or four of Hancock's cowpunchers were lounging in the doorway of the ranch house. He shouldered brusquely through them, and went on into the parlor of the house, where Hancock lay on the couch, as usual, with his rum-punch fixings on the table beside him. He took off his glasses as Mortimer entered, resettled them on his nose, and then smote his paunch a resounding whack.

'Ah, Harry!' he cried. 'You're the one soul in the world that I want to see. I don't mean about battering some of the Miller boys in Poplar Springs. That'll do your reputation on the range some good, though. Tackling guns with bare hands is rather a novelty in this part of the world, of course.... But what's that to me? Do you know what has meaning to me, Harry?'

Mortimer picked up the rum bottle, poured a swallow into a clean glass, and tossed it off. He said quietly, 'What makes a difference to you, Charles?' and his eyes hunted the body of

Hancock as though he were looking for a place to strike home a knife.

But Hancock was unaware of this. A wave of thought had overcome him, and memory dimmed his eyes as he said, 'I'm going to tell you something, my lad. I'm going to tell you about a woman.... Mind you, Harry, it was years ago.... But when I say "a woman", I want you to understand "*the* woman." Rare. Sudden. Something too beautiful to last.... Are you following me?'

'I follow you,' Mortimer said.

The rancher had almost closed his eyes as he consulted the picture from the past.

'I saw her. I adored her. I asked her to marry me. When she accepted me, Harry, the sound of her voice lifted me almost out of my boots. I went away planning my path through the world. And when I was about to take the prize in my hand, Harry – mark this – when I was about to take her to the church, she disappeared. Gone. Vanished absolutely. The way you say this range soil will vanish when the wind hits it just right. What took her away? A little wizened son of a French marquis with no more man in him than there is skin on the heel of my hand. She was gone. Lost to me. Love. Hope. What the hell will you have? She was all that!

'And since that day I've lain here with the rum bottle wondering how the devil I could get back at the whole female race. Can't do anything with them when you lie flat and simply think, because thought, on the whole, is beyond their ken. And therefore I had to wait until you did it for me. D'you see? You show me how women can be handled as easily as they handle men. Love her? *No!* Admire her? *No!* You simply take the woman and put her in your pocket. Who's the girl? Some cheap little chit? No, the best in the land. The proudest. The highest. The top of everything.... I stood here, last night, and saw her eyes melt when your name was mentioned. I saw the whole lovesick story come swooning into her face. And as a result of what? As a result of one evening of work. Why, Harry, when I saw what you had done, I wanted to get down on my knees and beg you for lessons.'

'So you told her everything, didn't you?' asked Mortimer.

Hancock took off a moment for thought. The wind, at the same moment, seemed to descend and grip the ranch house with a firmer hand. The whine of the storm ascended the scale by several notes.

'Told her?' said Hancock. 'I don't think that I told her anything. I couldn't say anything. I could only lie here and laugh. And admire you, Harry, and think how you'd paid off my score. And I want to tell you something, Harry. As I lay here last night I felt a deathless debt – gratitude, and all that. Wonderful feeling, Harry. The first time I've had it in my life. Absolutely extraordinary.'

'I dare say,' muttered Mortimer through his teeth.

'And that's why I'm glad to see you today,' said Hancock. 'Not because you've beaten eight of Miller's best men with your hands, but because you've subdued one woman, opened her heart, put tears in her eyes, made her knees tremble, when you didn't give a hang for her from the first to the last.' He broke into a gigantic peal of laughter which wound up on a gasping and spluttering.

'Close, in here,' said Hancock. 'Cool, but close, and that's strange, isn't it?'

Mortimer could not speak, seeing again the beauty and the pride of the girl who was lost to him.

'Chuck the door open, like a good fellow, will you?' asked Hancock. 'I never had so much trouble breathing. Is the alcohol getting me at last? Well, let it get me. I'll die laughing. I've seen the proud females, the high females, the pure females paid off for me, shot for shot. And I owe that to you, old fellow. Mortimer, I'll love you as long as I last!'

Mortimer went to the door and threw it wide. It seemed to him that ghosts rushed up into the lamplight, into his face. Then it was as though dim horses were galloping past in endless procession, and swifter than horses ever put hoof to the ground. He squinted his eyes into the dimness before he could understand that the swift whirl was a dust storm rushing past him at full

86

speed; the range itself was melting away before his eyes.

THREE

A flying arm of dust enveloped Mortimer and set him coughing as he closed the door and turned back into the room.

Hancock was grinning cheerfully. 'There she blows, Harry,' he said. 'There comes the dust storm you've been talking about for two years. Now we'll see if you've buttoned the topsoil down with all your plantings and plowings. Now we'll see if the range *has* been overgrazed, as you say, and what part of it is going to blow away.'

'That dust is blowing from far away,' said Mortimer. 'There isn't enough edge to this wind to tear up the ground badly. It will have to blow.'

The house trembled, as though nudged by an enormous shoulder, and the storm screamed an octave higher. The two men stared at each other; then Mortimer pulled out a bandanna and began to knot it around his throat.

'Get your hand-picked cowpunchers on the job, Charlie,' he suggested.

'It's dark, brother,' said Hancock, 'and the kind of lads I have don't work in the night.'

'All right,' said Mortimer. 'The cattle I save will be my share of the stock, and the dead ones can belong to you.'

He left the room with Hancock shouting loudly, 'Wait a minute, Harry! All for one and one for all ...'

When Mortimer stepped into the open the gale was blowing hard enough to set his eyelids trembling. It came at him like a river of darkness. He bumped the corner of the house, turning toward the barracks shed, and then the wind caught him from the side and set him staggering.

The light in the window of the shed was a dull, greenish blur. He had to fumble to find the door, and he pressed his way in, to find a jingling of pots and pans in the kitchen and the CCC men sneezing and cursing in the mist which filtered rapidly through the cracks in the walls of the shed. They stood up and looked silently toward him for an explanation.

He said, 'It's the dust storm, boys. Pulled at my feet like water.... No man has to go out into weather like this, but if any of you volunteer to give a hand ...'

Jan Erickson turned his head slowly to survey the group. 'Leave me see the man that *won't* volunteer,' he said ominously.

But not one of them hung back. They were a solid unit, and a speechless content filled Mortimer's heart, till Shorty appeared in the kitchen door, shouting, 'There's gunna be plenty of grit in the flour bin and mud in the coffee, Chief!'

A louder howling of the wind seemed to answer Shorty directly and set the men laughing. They equipped themselves as Mortimer directed, with shirts buttoned close at neck and wrist to keep out the flying sand, and with bandannas ready to pull up over mouth and nose. A big canteen to each should give enough water to wash the mouth clean for a few hours and keep the bandanna wet in case it were necessary to strain the dust out more thoroughly. Four of them would ride with Charlie Hancock's cowpunchers to help handle the cattle, which probably were drifting rapidly before the storm and lodging helpless against the fencelines. The thing to do was to get the weakest of the livestock into the barns and round up the mass of them in the Chappany Valley, where Mortimer's young groves of trees would give some shelter against the whip of the wind and the drifting of the soil. It was true that all this work properly belonged to Hancock's cowpunchers, but under Mortimer's control the CCC men had learned every detail of the ranch work long ago.

They went out with Mortimer now and worked all night.

The wind kept coming like a thousand devils out of the northwest, and into the southeast, at the farthest limit of the Hancock land, Mortimer led a group of the CCC men. They found two hundred steers drifted against a barbed wire fence, with their heads down and the drift sand already piled knee-deep around them. There they would remain until the sand heaped over them in a great dune. It required hard work to turn the herd, shooting guns in their faces, shouting and flogging, but at last it began to move back towards the Chappany Valley.

Streaks and slitherings of moonlight that got through the hurly-burly showed the cattle continually drifting aslant, to turn their faces from the storm. It was like riding into a sandblast. In five minutes a fine silt had forced its way under tight wristbands and down the collars of the punchers, so that a crawling discomfort possessed their bodies. Dust was thick on every tongue, and there was a horrible sense of the lungs filling, so that breathing was more labored, though less air got to the blood.

When they had jammed those steers into the Chappany, letting them drink on the way at the lowest of the two Hancock lakes, they pushed the herd into one of the groves of trees which Mortimer had planted two years before. The slant of the ground gave some protection. The spindling trees by their multitude afforded a fence which seemed to whip and filter the air somewhat cleaner. Even that push against the dusty wind had been almost too much for some of the cattle. A good many of them did not mill at all, but slumped to their knees. The others, wandering, lowing, and bellowing, pooled up around the steers that went down, and presently the entire herd was holding well. But some of those that went down would be dead before morning.

It was not a time to count small losses, however. It was like riding out a storm in an old, cranky, and helpless ship. The cargo hardly mattered. Life was the thing to consider.

Mortimer washed out his nose and throat from his canteen and moistened the bandanna which covered the lower part of his face. He sent his contingent of riders back to find more fence-lodged cattle and aimed his own tough cow pony at a dim twinkle of lanterns high up across the valley, above the three Miller lakes. He could guess what those lights indicated, and the picture of disaster bulked suddenly in his mind greater and blacker than the storm itself.

He took the way straight up the valley, however, and rode the slope toward Miller's thousand acres of plowed ground. Heading into the wind, in this manner, it was impossible to keep the eyes open very long at a time. No matter how narrowly he squinted, the fine silt blew through the lashes and tormented the eyeballs.

He had to pick direction from time to time, checking the pony's efforts to turn its head from the torment; otherwise he kept his eyes fast shut.

There were two square miles of that plowed and hay-covered cropland. He came up on the northern edge of it and found the mustang stepping on hard, smooth ground. When he used his flashlight, he saw that the border acres which edged toward the wind had blown away like a dream. The reddish hardpan, tough as burned bricks, was all that remained!

He dismounted, tried to clear his throat, and found that the choke of the dust storm had penetrated to the bottom of his lungs like thick smoke. Panic stormed up in his brain. He beat the terror down and went about his observations. There were things to see, here, which should be reported exactly in the notebook that was his source of information to be sent to the government.

It was a dark moment of the storm, for the wind came on with a scream and a steel-edge whistling through the hay, and the moon was shut away almost entirely. It merely showed in the sky vague tumblings and shapeless rollings of dust that seemed to spill more loosely across the heavens than mere clouds ever do; and sometimes it was as though the earth had exploded and the results of the explosion were hanging motionless in the air. But what he wanted to see was far more intimately close at hand.

He went over the bared ground to the rim of the yet standing hay. In places it was rolled back and heaped like matting; sometimes it gathered in cone-shaped masses like shocked hay; but every now and then the wind got its finger tips under the shocks and the rolls and blew them to smithereens with a single breath. On his knees Mortimer turned the flashlight on the edge of the hayland and watched the action of the storm. At that point the life-sustaining humus was about a foot deep to the hardpan. The top portion, which had been loosened by the plow, ran down from four to six inches, and this part gave way rapidly, sifting from around the white roots of the hay until each stalk, at the end, was suddenly jerked away. In the meantime, the scouring blast worked more gradually at the lower, unplowed layer of the soil, which was compacted with the fine, hairlike roots of the range grass. Even this gave way with amazing rapidity.

The hayland was doomed. An army working hand to hand, could not have saved it. As he mounted, the swinging ray of the electric torch showed Mortimer another horseman who sat the saddle not far away, impassive. The long-legged horse kept picking up its feet nervously and making small bucking movements of protest, but the rider held it like a pitching boat in a rough sea. Mortimer, coming nearer, saw the masked face and the sand-reddened eyes of John Miller, who was watching twelve thousand dollars' worth of hay and fifty thousand irreplaceable dollars' worth of topsoil blow to hell. Impassive, by the ragged glimpses of light which the moon offered, the rancher stared at the quick destruction. Mortimer rode to his side and shouted, 'Sorry, Miller!'

John Miller gave him a silent glance, and then resumed his study of the growing ruin before him. Mortimer turned his mustang back into the Chappany Valley.

He passed over a long stretch of the Miller bottom land which had been plowed for onions and potatoes. The deep, black soil was withering away into pock-marks, or dissolving under the breath of the storm. Mortimer groaned as he paused to watch the steady destruction. That heavy loam had formed centuries or hundreds of centuries before among the roots of the forested uplands. Rain had washed it gradually into the rivers. The Chappany floods had spread it over the flat of the valley lands. And this rich impost which nature had spread in ten thousand careful layers was blowing headlong away, forever! It seemed to Mortimer that all America was vanishing from beneath his feet.

He hurried on down the Chappany, looking again and again, anxiously, toward the flickering line of lanterns that shone from the high ground above the Miller lakes. He had warned Miller two years ago, by word and by example, about the danger of those rolling sand dunes, above the bluff. If a great wind came from this quarter, the whole mass of sand might come to life like water and spill over the edge of the bluff to fill the lakes beneath and sponge up the priceless water.

Then the wind came down the Chappany Valley like dark water rushing through a flume, and the lanterns were dimmed.

Out of the sweeping dimness, which sometimes blew his horse sliding, he came back onto the Hancock land and dismounted. With his flashlight he studied half a mile of terrain. On one side, some contour-plowing was commencing to blow a little, but, everywhere else he looked, his trees, his stretches of shrubbery over exposed shoulders, and the tough grasses with wide-spreading roots which he had planted were buttoning the soil to the hardpan, holding the ground like a green overcoat of varying textures.

One shouting burst of triumph filled his throat, but after that the joy slipped away from him and left his heart cold. For somehow his soul had struck roots in the whole countryside. Now hundreds of thousands of good acres all over the range were threatened, and it seemed to Mortimer that children of his body, not the mere hopes of his mind and the planned future, were imperiled.

He turned his horse up the slope, where the

bluff diminished to a reasonable slope. Off to the left the headlights of an automobile came bucking through the dimness. A great truck went by him, roaring, with a load of long timbers.

Mortimer's heart sank, for he knew the meaning of that. He spurred the mustang on behind the lighted path of the truck until he reached the sand dunes immediately above the two long lakes which belonged on the Hancock land and held water for the Hancock cattle.

The sand which came on the whistling wind, up there, cut at the skin and endangered the eyes, but his flashlight showed him no portion of the Hancock dunes wearing under the storm! From the edge of the bluff and back for a hundred yards, he had planted a tough Scotch scrub which had the look of heather, though it never bloomed. For fuel it was useless. No cattle would graze on those bitter, varnished leaves. That shrubbery served no purpose in the world except to shield the ground under it. It grew not more than a foot high, but it spread in such solid masses that wind could not get at its roots.

Behind the shrubbery he had planted fifty rows of tough saplings, close as a fence. They had grown slowly, but the thickened trunks stood up now like solidly built palings against the storm. Beyond them, and stretching as far as the dunes rolled into the back country, Mortimer had covered every inch of the ground with a grass from the Russian steppes, where eight months of the year the earth is frozen, and where for four months this close-growing, stubborn grass covers the soil like a blanket of a fine weave and offers a steady pasturage for wandering herds of small cattle. For two years it had been rooting and spreading, and now it clothed the dunes behind the Hancock lakes with an impermeable vesture. The dunes themselves had been anchored, here, but the flying silt which filled the air was banking up outside the farther lines of his fence of saplings. It was conceivable that if the storm continued for days it might gradually heap the wave of sand so high that the trees would be overwhelmed; but little of the sweeping sand could ever roll over the bluff and drop into the lakes beneath.

Once more the triumph went with a riot through Mortimer's blood; and once more the triumph died suddenly away as he looked at the lanterns that stretched before him along the edge of the bluff.

There were far more lights than he had expected; and, now that he came closer, he found two hundred men laboring in a mist of blow-sand. Orders, yelled from time to time, sang on the wind and vanished suddenly. Here and there men were down on their knees, work forgotten as they tried to cough the dust out of their lungs.

Of course, the Miller ranch could not supply

such a force of working hands as this. The men were from all the adjacent range. For the first sweep of the storm had choked a thousand pools with silt and had begun to damage the water in many a standing tank. The small ranchers in such a time of need turned naturally toward John Miller, but, when they telephoned, the ominous answer was that the dunes were crawling in slow waves toward the edge of the bluff above the lakes which served as reservoirs, during the dry season, not only for Miller's cattle but for the herds of his neighbors. That news brought men from all of the vicinity. The trucks of the Miller place carried timbers to the bluff. And the entire army was slaving to erect a fence that would halt the slow drift of the dunes. To fence off the whole length of the three lakes was impossible, so they selected the largest of the three, the one just above the Hancock property line, and here a double fence-line was being run.

John Miller himself appeared on the scene at this time and commenced to ride up and down, giving advice, snapping brief orders. He looked to Mortimer like a resolute general in the midst of a battle, but this was a losing fight.

For the whole backland, the whole retiring sweep of the dunes was rising up in a smother of blow-sand, heaping loosely spilling masses on the ridges of the dunes, so that there was a constantly forward flow as though of incredibly reluctant

100

waves. And the piling weight of that sand was as heavy as water, also.

The men worked with a sullen, patient endurance, scooping out footholds for the posts, boarding them across, with interstices between the boards, and then supporting the shaky structure against the sweep of wind and the roll of sand with long, angled shorings.

One woman moved up and down the line with a bucket of water and a sponge. As she came near, the workers raised the handkerchiefs which covered nose and mouth. Some of them stood with open mouth and tongue thrust out to receive the quick swabbing with water that enabled them to breathe again. Mortimer saw that it was Louise Miller, masked herself, like a gypsy. He swung down from his horse and laid hold of the bail of the bucket.

'I'll handle this, Lou,' he told her. 'It's too heavy a job for you—'

Weariness had unsteadied her, and the wind staggered her heavily against Mortimer. So, for an instant, she let her weight lean against him. Then she pulled up the bandanna that covered her face.

'It's a great day for you!' she gasped. 'We laughed at you, did we? We wouldn't listen when you talked sense to us? Well, it's the turn for the dirt doctor to laugh while the whole range blows away from under our feet.'

He picked up the sponge from the soupy water of the pail and swabbed off the sand and black muck from her face. He steadied her with one hand against the wind while he did it.

She sneered, 'We're learning our lesson. If the wind leaves us anything, we'll get down on our knees and ask you to teach us how to keep it.'

He passed the sponge over her face again. 'You're talking like a fool, a little, spoiled fool,' he said.

She answered through her teeth: 'Get off our land and stay off. We'd rather let the wind blow us all the way to hell than have you lift a hand to help us.'

She caught up the pail and went on, walking more swiftly, though the sand dripped and blew from about her feet as they lifted from the soft ground.

John Miller came up, fighting his horse into the wind, when a kneeling, coughing figure jumped up suddenly from the ground and gripped the reins of Miller's horse under the bit. With his other hand he gestured wildly toward Mortimer.

'You wouldn't listen to him!' screamed the rancher. 'You *knew!* You laughed at him. You knew *every*thing! He was only a fool tenderfoot. And God gave all the sense to the Millers! ... But look at the Hancock place; look at the safe water; and then look at *you!* Damn you for a fake and a fool! I hope you rot!' He dropped to the ground again, and began trying once more to cough the dust from his lungs.

Miller drove his horse up to Mortimer. 'You've got three men working with us here,' he said. 'Take them away. We don't need their hands. We don't need your brains. Get off the Miller land!'

Mortimer turned without a word of protest, letting his horse drift before the wind. He found Lefty Parkman and gave him the order to leave the work, together with the other two. They trooped back toward the Hancock place with their chief, and, as they went, Mortimer took grim notice of how the first sand fence was already sagging under the irresistible weight of accumulating silt. But the whole storm and the fate of the entire range had become a smaller thing to him since his last glimpse of Lou Miller. The pain of it lingered under his heart like the cold of a sword. It was not the blow-sand that kept him from drawing breath, but the fine, poisonous dust of grief.

Then the thought of Hancock and how the fat drunkard had betrayed him blinded his eyes with anger. He drove the snorting mustang ahead of his men and rushed to the ranch house. The thickest smother of the storm was coiling around him as he broke in through the doorway to the hall.

Then, as he turned from the hall toward the entrance to the parlor, he heard Hancock singing cheerfully to himself, and saw the man stretched as usual on the couch with the rum punch beside him.

'Hi, Harry!' called Charlie Hancock. 'How's the little sand-blow? Been a hero again, old boy? Charmed any more girls off the tree?'

It seemed to Mortimer, as he blinked his sore eyes, that he was looking through an infinite distance of more than space and time toward his ranching partner. The rage that had been building in him sank away to a dumb disgust. Then the telephone at the end of the room began to purr.

'For you,' said Hancock. 'This thing has been ringing all night. The world seems to want Harry Mortimer, after forgetting him all these years.'

Over the wire a strident, nasal voice said, 'Mortimer? This is Luke Waterson over in Patchen Valley.... The wind's blowing hell out of things, over here.... Barn's gone down, slam! Forty head inside it. Mortimer, I don't care about barns and cattle, but the ground's whipping away from under our feet. You're an expert about that. You claim you can keep the ground buttoned down tight. For God's sake tell us what to do. We'll all pitch in and wear our hands to the bone if you'll tell me how to start ...'

Mortimer said, 'Waterson, it makes my heart ache to hear you. God knows that I'd help you if I could. But the only way to anchor the topsoil is to use time as well as thought and ...'

104

'You mean that you won't tell me the answer?' shouted Waterson.

'There's no answer I can give when ...' began Mortimer. But he heard the receiver slammed up at the other end.

As he turned away from the phone, it rang again with a long clamor.

'This is Tom Knight. Down at Pokerville,' said another voice. 'Mortimer, I've always been one of the few that believed you knew your business. And now the devil is to pay down here. Sand and silt in all three of our tanks. No water. But that's nothing. I've got three hundred acres in winter wheat and, by God, it's blowing into the sky! Mortimer, what can I do to hold the soil? It's going through my fingers like water through a sieve ...'

'I can't tell you, Mr. Knight,' called Mortimer. 'You need two years of careful planting, and less crowding on the cattle range ...'

'Two years? Hell, man, I'm talking about hours, not years! In twenty-four hours there won't be enough grass on my lands to feed a frog! Can you give me the answer?'

'Not even God could help your land till the wind stops blowing, Mr Knight ...'

'Damn you and your books and your theories, then!' roared Knight. And his receiver crashed on the hook.

The instrument was hardly in place when the bell rang again.

105

'Take it, Charlie, will you?' asked Mortimer weakly.

'I'll take it. *I'll* tell 'em,' said Hancock.

He strode to the telephone and presently was shouting into the mouthpiece, '... and even if he were here I wouldn't let him waste time on you. For two years he's been trying to show you the way out. You knew too much to listen. Stay where you are and choke with dust, or else come up here and see how the Hancock acres are sticking fast to the hardpan!' He laughed as he hung up.

'That's the way to talk to 'em,' he said. 'You're in the saddle now. You've been ridiculed and ostracised for two years. Now let 'em taste the spur. Ram it into 'em and give the rowels a twist.... I wish I had 'em where *you* have 'em. They've sneered at drunken Charlie Hancock all these years. I'd make 'em dizzy if I had the chance, now. I'd tell 'em how to ...'

Mortimer escaped from the tirade. He was still weak, as though after a great shock. Sometimes he found himself wondering at the hollowness in his heart, and at the pain, which was like homesickness and fear of battle combined. But then he remembered the girl and the strain of her lips as she denounced him.

He went out into the howl and darkness of the storm for sheer relief.

For forty-eight hours he worked without closing his eyes. Even Jan Erickson broke down before that and lay on the floor of the barracks shed on his back, uttering a snoring sound in his throat though his eyes were wide open, and a black drool ran from the corner of his mouth. Pudge Major developed a sort of asthma. His throat and his entire face swelled. He lay on his bed propped up into the only position in which he could breathe.

Mortimer gave the Chinaman twenty dollars to spend every spare moment at Pudge's bedside; his own place had to be outside, for greater events were happening every hour.

In the middle of the second day of that unrelenting wind, the last defense on top of the bluff gave way and the sand began to flood down into the third of Miller's lakes. The first two had choked up within twenty-four hours of the start of the blow. The backed-up heights of the flowing sand quickly overwhelmed the third. In the thick, horrible dusk cattle were seen, mad with thirst, thrusting their muzzles deep into the wet ooze, stifling, dying in the muck.

That was when John Miller came up to the Hancock house. It happened, at this moment, that Mortimer had dropped into the barracks shed to see the progress of poor Pudge Major and had found him slightly improved. While he was there Wang appeared, coming from the house with incredible speed.

He gave the word that the great man of the range was in the ranch house, and Mortimer went instantly into the parlor of the main building. He found Hancock with his face more swollen and rum-reddened than ever, and in the same half-dressed condition, while Miller, with ten years added to his age, sat with a steaming glass of punch in his hand. He stood up when Mortimer entered.

'He wants help,' said Hancock. His savage exultation at this surrender of his old enemy made him clip the words short. 'I have the vote on this ranch,' he added. 'I have the two-thirds interest behind me, but I want your opinion, Mortimer. Shall we let the Miller cattle water in our lakes? Shall we charge 'em a dollar a head, or is it *safe* to let them use up our reserve supply at any price?'

Mortimer watched the rancher take these humiliating blows with an unmoved face.

'It is true,' said Miller, 'that I am on my knees. I'm begging for water, Mr. Mortimer. Shall I have it?'

'You want it for your own cattle and you want it for those of your friends?' said Mortimer.

'Too many. Can't do it,' said Hancock, shaking his head.

'I would be ashamed to get water for my own cattle and not for the herds of my neighbors,' said Miller. 'Some of us have lived on the range like brothers for several generations.'

'I'm not of that brotherhood, Miller,' snapped

Hancock. He added, 'Can't water the cows of every man under the sky. Can't and won't. There isn't enough in my lakes.'

'I put six feet on each of our dams last year,' said Mortimer.

'Perhaps you did,' said Hancock, 'but still there's not enough to ...'

'There's enough water there for the whole community,' said Mortimer. 'We've backed up three times as much ...'

'If they get water, they'll pay for it,' said Hancock. 'Business, Miller. Business is the word between us. Do you remember five years ago when I wanted to run a road across that southeastern corner of your place?'

'That was my foreman's work,' said Miller. 'I was not on the place when he refused you.'

'Why didn't you change his mind for him when you got back, then?' demanded Hancock.

'You didn't ask a second time,' said the old rancher.

'Ah, you thought I'd come and crawl to you, did you?' asked Hancock. 'But I'm not that sort. It doesn't run in the Hancock blood to come crawling.... And now I'll tell you what I'll do. I'll let your cows come to my water; but they'll pay a dollar a head for each day spent beside the lakes. Understand? A dollar a head.'

Miller said nothing. His lips pinched hard together.

'This drought may last two weeks, a month,'

said Mortimer, 'before the water holes are cleaned out and before trenches catch the seepage from the choked lakes. The people around here won't pay thirty dollars to water their cows for a month.'

'They won't pay? They will, though,' said Hancock. 'They *won't* pay? I want to see them get one drop of water without handing me cash for it!'

Miller took a deep breath and replaced his untasted glass on the table.

'I think you know what this means, Hancock,' he said. 'There are some impatient men waiting at my house, now. When I tell them what you have to say, I think they're apt to come and get the water they need, in spite of you.'

'My dear Miller,' said Hancock, 'I occasionally have a glass, as perhaps you and the rotten gossips know, but my hand is still steady.' He held out his glass. The liquid stood as steady as a painted color inside it. 'I've lost touch with the rest of the world, but my rifle remains my very good friend,' said Hancock. 'When you and your friends come over, you can have what you wish: water or blood, or both. But for the water you'll pay.'

Miller looked carefully at his host for a moment. Then he turned and left the room in silence.

When he was gone, Hancock threw up a fist and shook it at the ceiling. 'Did you hear me, Harry?' he demanded. 'Did I tell it to him? Did I pour it down his throat? … Oh, God, I've waited fifteen years to show the range that I'm a man, and now that they're beginning to find it out, they'll keep on finding. Harry, hell is going to pop, and at last I'll be in the middle of it. Not a rum-stew, but a man-sized hell of my own making!'

Argument would have been, of all follies, the most complete. Mortimer sat in a corner of the room with a glass of straight rum and felt it burning the rawness of his throat as he watched Hancock pull on riding clothes. A heavy cartridge belt slanted around his hips, with a big automatic weighting it down on one side. He put on a sombrero and pulled a chin band down to keep it firmly in place. Then he picked up his repeating rifle, and laughed.

A siren began to sound above the house at the same time. It would bring back to the ranch house those fighting cow hands of whom Hancock was so proud and who owed their existence out of jail to his generosity and careless fondness for their bad records in the past. The sound of that siren, cutting through the whirl of the wind, would tell the true story to John Miller as he journeyed back to his ranch. And Mortimer could foretell the great cleaning of guns and gathering of ammunition which would reply to it.

He heard Hancock saying, 'Harry, in a sense it's all owing to you. I've had mental indigestion most of my life because a girl smacked me down. Except for you there'd be choked lakes for Hancock as well as for Miller. But, as it is, I have the bone that the dog will jump for, and I'm going to hold it high! Are you with me?'

'Quit it, Charlie, will you?' said Mortimer. 'You think you're showing yourself a man. You're not. You're being a baby in a tantrum.'

'Before this baby gets through squalling,' said Hancock, 'a lot of big, strong men on this range are going to wish that I never was born. Before I'm through ...'

A hand knocked; the front door pushed open, and a slight figure that staggered into the hallway in a whirl of dust now looked into the living-room with the face of Lou Miller. With her eyes wind-bleared and her hat dragged to the side, and weariness making her walk with a shambling step, she should have looked like nothing worth a second glance; instead, she seemed to Mortimer to be shaped and God-given specially to fill his heart. Her eyes found him and forgot him in the first instant. She said to Hancock, 'My father came to talk business, I know. But he didn't get far, did he?'

'Not one step, Lou,' said Hancock.

'Father came to talk business,' she said. 'But I've come to beg.'

'You?' said Hancock. 'You're Miller's daughter. You can't beg.'

'On my knees, if it will do any good,' said the girl.

112

'Did *he* send you here?' asked Hancock, with malicious curiosity.

'He doesn't know that I'm here. But if you'll give us a chance I'll let the whole world know the kindness that's in you, Charlie,' she told him.

'Ah, quit all that,' said Hancock.

'Charlie, will you listen to me?' she pleaded.

He began to walk up and down and she followed him, trying to stop him with her gestures.

'They've always smacked me down. By God! If they get anything out of me now, they'll have to fight for it,' he said.

'It can't come to that. God won't let it come to that. Not on this range,' said the girl. She began to cry, and struck herself across the mouth to keep back the sobbing. 'And don't think about the humans. Let's admit that we're a rotten lot, all of us. But think of the poor beasts, Charlie! They're wedged against the fences. The sand is drifting them down. I shone a flashlight across ten thousand pairs of eyes that were dying. Charlie, are you listening to me?'

She pulled softly at his arm, but Hancock was staring up at the ceiling.

'You know something?' he said. 'Back there when I was alive – back there before I turned into rum-bloat and poison ivy, if you'd lifted a finger you wouldn't have had to ask. I would have given you my blood – look – like this – like soup. But the way it is now, I'm finished. I'm going to get one

113

thing out of tonight, and that's a chance to die in a scrap.'

'Don't say that!' she cried out. She stood up on tiptoe, trying to look him in the eye and make him answer her, mind to mind. But he kept his eyes on the ceiling.

He said, 'It's no good. Not if you were Sheba and Cleopatra. I'm cooked. I'm finished. But when they bury me they're going to know that I was a man. Lou, get out. I won't talk any more.'

'I've *got* to talk,' said the girl. 'If you go ahead, there'll be murder in the Chappany.'

'Get out or I'll smack you down,' said Hancock, looking at the ceiling.

It had been an agony to Mortimer. He took the girl by the arm and made her go into the hall with him. 'You can't go home just yet,' he said. 'You're as weak and full of wobbles as a new calf. You can't head off into this wind.'

She leaned against him for a moment, silently gathering strength, and then pushed herself away. She had not met his eyes once; she did not meet them now as she went to the outer door. Mortimer put his hand on its knob.

'Look here,' he said, 'I'm not a coyote or a hydrophobia skunk. You came up and let Hancock talk to you the other day. But what he told you isn't the whole truth. Will you let me speak?'

'I'll go now,' she answered.

'I haven't a right to let you go out and be choked

114

in the dust,' said Mortimer.

'I'd rather be choked there than here,' she told him. 'Let me go.'

'Sickens you, doesn't it?' asked Mortimer, trying to find something in her face.

'I'll tell you one thing,' she said, staring straight before her. 'There wasn't any hatred in the Chappany Valley till you came. There was love!' Her voice broke. 'We all loved one another. We were happy—'

He said nothing. She made a gesture to indicate that the breaking of her voice meant nothing. Then she added, with a sudden savagery, 'You're from the outside – all of you. Why didn't you stay out? Why don't you go away?'

He felt the words from his heart to his forehead, where a cold pain settled. Then he pulled the door open and took her outside. Her horse had crowded against the house, head down. He helped her into the saddle and saw horse and girl reel as she swung off into the wind. A moment later the darkness ate them up.

He turned and went back into the house.

'Will you listen to me?' asked Mortimer.

'I'll hear no arguments,' said Hancock. 'Now that I'm started I want what lies ahead. You can't turn me, brother!'

Mortimer stood up and tightened his belt a notch. The fatigue which had been growing as a weight in his brain gradually melted away and a cold, clear river of forethought flowed through him. 'I think you mean business, Charlie,' he said.

'I mean it with my whole heart,' said Hancock.

'Do you think your father would approve of this? Would old Jim Hancock refuse water to the cows of his neighbors?' asked Mortimer.

'Old Jim Hancock is an old fool,' said Charlie. 'And he's fifteen miles away in Poplar Springs. Who's going to get to him to ask how he votes on the business? The roads are wind-worn into badlands or else they're drifted belly-deep in silt and sand. Nobody will get to him for a fortnight. And the dance will be over before that.'

'Do you know what it will mean?' asked Mortimer.

'I suppose it means *that*, to begin with,' said Hancock.

He raised a finger for silence, and Mortimer heard it coming down the wind, a long-drawn-out, organlike moaning, or as though all the stops of the organ had been opened, from the shrillest treble to the deepest bass. That was the lowing of the thirst-stricken cattle which milled beyond the fences of the Hancock place, held from their search for water.

Hancock smiled as he listened. 'There it is,' he said. 'The mob's on the stage. They're calling to Oedipus. They want the king. They're waiting for the main actor!' He laughed.

Mortimer struck him across the face with the

flat of his hand. He intended it more as a gesture than a blow, but he hit with more force than he had intended, and Hancock staggered.

'Don't reach for that gun,' said Mortimer.

'No,' said Hancock calmly. 'I know that you could break my back for me.'

'I had to say something to you. Words weren't any good,' remarked Mortimer.

'Ah, you think the ship is about to sink, do you?' asked Hancock, with an ugly twist of his loose mouth. 'You think it's time for the rats to leave. Is that it?'

Mortimer said, 'I came out here on the range to do something that the range didn't want. All I managed to accomplish was to put a prize in your hand that's worth a fight.... Are you hearing me, Hancock?'

'With an extreme and curious interest,' said Charles Hancock.

'I'm not an expert shot,' said Mortimer.

'You're very good if you take time and put your mind on it,' admitted Hancock. 'The making of a real expert.'

'Well, Charlie,' said Mortimer, 'if you kill a man attempting to get his cattle to your water, I'll manage to come to you afterward. You may put the first three bullets into me, Charlie, but I'll kill you as surely as there's wind in the sky.'

They eyed each other with a profound and steady interest.

117

'Is that all?' asked Hancock.

Mortimer went out of the house and into the barracks shed. He said to Shorty, 'You stay here with Pudge Major. As the rest of the boys come in, send them after me to the Miller place.'

'Send them *where*?' shouted Shorty.

'To the Miller place,' said Mortimer, and went to the barn.

Mortimer did not take a horse from the group of saddle stock which had been tethered in the barn. Instead, he selected a ten-year-old Missouri mule, Chico, with a potbelly that meant as much to his endurance as the fat hump means to the camel, with a lean, scrawny neck, with a head as old as Methuselah's, filled with wicked wisdom, and with four flawless legs and four hoofs of impenetrable iron.

Then Mortimer started the voyage across the Chappany Valley toward the Miller house.

The sky closed with darkness above him when he was halfway across the valley, and he had to put up his bandanna over nose and mouth, as before, to make breathing possible in that continuous smother. The wisdom of Chico, recognizing a trail, enabled the rider to keep his eyes shut most of the way. He opened them to squint, from time to time, at the drifted silt in the valley floor and the bare patches of good grass on the Hancock land, where he had planted the holding coverage to protect the soil.

118

Here and there, across the Hancock range, acres had given way and blown off like a thought; but the great mass of the soil had held firmly, because for two years he had been covering the weak spots, with a religious zeal. Wherever he had worked, the victory went to him, but it was small consolation. There would be blood on the land before long, he was sure. And in some strange measure that was also his work. But always, as he rode, the sense of irretrievable loss accompanied him, and that hollowness grew in his heart, and that endless defeat. He had acted out with care one great lie in his entire life, and though in the end he had found that it was not acting, but the very truth of his soul, he knew that the girl would never forgive him.

When he got to the Miller place he found automobiles and trucks parked everywhere, with sand drifted body-high around many of them. The patio entrance was three feet deep in drift, and when he reached the interior and tethered Chico to one of the old iron rings that surrounded the court, he stood for a moment and listened to the wind, to the mourning of the cattle down the Chappany, and to the nearer sound of angry voices inside the big house. After that, he entered the place. The uproar came from the big library. He went straight to it and stood winking the grit from his eyes and looking from the threshold over the crowd.

There were fifty men in the room, and none of them were mere cowpunchers. These were the assembled heads of the ranches of the surrounding district, and they meant swift, bitter business. Hancock, if he used guns, would not live long enough for Mortimer to get at him. These armed men would attend to him quickly, and forever.

The whole noise of the argument rolled away into silence as Mortimer showed himself.

John Miller came halfway across the room toward him with quick steps. He said, 'Mr. Mortimer, no man has ever been ordered to leave my house before, but in your case ...'

Mortimer put up a weary hand. 'I'm tired of your pride,' he said. 'I've come over here to see if I can stop murder. Will you listen to me?'

Miller said nothing. He was reaching into his mind for some adequate answer when a gray-headed man said, 'Let's be open about it, Miller. He's younger than we are. He's a tenderfoot. But I've been over some of the Hancock land, and I've seen it holding like a rock. Who made it hold? This fellow did. Give him a dash of credit, and for God's sake let's hear what he has to say. Maybe we have to begin ranching with the A B Cs again; maybe he's to be our teacher.'

Mortimer said, 'Gentlemen, a dollar a head is what Hancock will ask for every head of cattle that waters on our place. That's a good deal of money, and I don't suppose you'll stand for it. If I

120

throw in my third of that dollar, it cuts the price down to sixty-seven cents. I wonder if that will make a sufficient difference to you. Will you do business with Hancock on that basis?'

They were silent as they listened to this proposal. Then John Miller said, 'I understand you donate your third of the spoils?'

'I donate it,' said Mortimer, and yawned. He was very tired.

Miller said, 'Suppose we call this emergency an act of God and refuse to pay a penny for the surplus which our neighbors may happen to have of what means life to all of us?'

'In that case,' said Mortimer wearily, 'I suppose I'm with you. I've sent for my men to follow me over here. I've told Hancock that if he shoots to kill I'll go for his throat.'

He got another silence for that speech. Someone said loudly, 'I thought you said that you knew this fellow, Miller?'

Miller answered in a harsh, strained voice, 'I seem to be a fool, Ollie. It's perfectly apparent that I don't know *any*thing.'

'If you try to rush cattle down to the lakes,' said Mortimer, 'you'll find Charlie Hancock and his men waiting for you, and every puncher on his place shoots straight. There are plenty of you to wipe them out, but there'll be a dozen men dead in the Chappany Valley before the business ends. Another dozen hours won't kill that many cattle out of all the herds that are waiting for water. Let me have that time to get through to Jim Hancock in Poplar Springs.'

John Miller came up to him with a bewildered face. 'You can't get through, Mortimer,' he argued. 'The trail's drifted across knee-deep with sand in a lot of places. I don't think a horse could live through fifteen miles of the dust storm, anyway.'

'A mule could, however,' said Mortimer.

'Suppose you managed by luck to get to Poplar Springs,' said Miller, 'you couldn't get a thing from old Jim Hancock. He hates me and the rest of the ranchers of this district. He doesn't give a hang for anything except a newspaper and a daily game of checkers. I know him like a book, and that's the truth. He'd laugh in your face. He'd rub his hands and warm them at the idea of a war in the Chappany Valley. Mortimer, will you believe me? Very gallant, this intention of yours, but entirely useless. You can't get to Poplar Springs, and, if you do, your trip will be useless.'

Mortimer said, 'Look at these men. They're a sour lot. They mean business. If you can't hold them for a few hours, they'll go down to rush Charlie Hancock's rifles. And dead men piled on one another will be all that I've gained from two years of work.... If I get to Jim Hancock I'll bring him back with me.'

'I can't let you go,' said Miller solemnly.

'I'll have to look at the tethering of my mule,'

said Mortimer. 'Then I'll come back and talk it over with you.'

A maid with a frightened face entered the room and said, 'Mr. Miller, I've been looking everywhere for Miss Louise. She's not in the house, sir. She's not anywhere.'

'Not in the house?' shouted Miller. 'Are you crazy? You mean she's out in this storm? ... Go up into the garret. She'll be there with some of her old gadgets. That's her playground, and she's nine tenths baby, still.'

Of that, Mortimer heard only a whisper that died behind him; he was too full of his own plans and problems. He went back into the patio, untied Chico, and rode out through the patio entrance. The dust-blast half blinded him, instantly, but he turned the mule across the sweep of the wind and headed Chico toward Poplar Springs.

FOUR

Mortimer got three miles of comparatively easy breathing to begin his journey. He saw the whole face of the countryside, sand-buried or sand-swept, and the trail recognizable from time to time, dots and dashes of it in the midst of obliteration.

He had passed the abandoned Carter place, with the sand heaped against the windward walls like shadows of brightness rather than dark, before the storm came at him again like a herd of sky-high elephants, throwing up their trunks and trampling the earth to black smoke. It sounded like a herd of elephants all trumpeting together. He thought he had seen the worst of the business before this, but that black boiling up of trouble was as thick as pitch.

He put his head down and endured, endlessly, while Chico, through that choking smother, found the dots and dashes of the disappearing trail with a faultless instinct. It seemed to Mortimer that the land was like a living body, now bleeding to death. The work of innumerable dead centuries was rushing about him like a nightmare.

Then Chico stumbled on something soft and shied. Mortimer turned the shaft of his pocket torch down through the murk and saw the body of a horse on the ground. It was Hampton. He knew it by the unforgettable streak of white, like a light on the forehead.

He dismounted. Sand was heaped along the back of the dead horse, half burying the body, but the tail blew out with an imitation of life along the wind. Sand filled the dead eyes. The left foreleg was broken below the knee. There was a round bullet hole above the temple that had brought quick death to the thoroughbred. What he guessed back there at Miller's house was true. Lou had headed for town, perhaps in hope of bringing back men of the law to restore peace to the Chappany Valley. She had stripped saddle and girth from Hampton. That meant she was somewhere not far away at this time, with the storm overwhelming her. The saddle would give her a bit of shelter and a shield behind which she could breathe.

He narrowed his eyes to the thinnest slit and held up his hands to turn the immediate edge of the wind, but the rolling darkness showed him only its own face as he rode the mule in circles around the dead body of Hampton. The electric torch was like a lance-shaft, a brittle thing that elongated or broke off short according to the density of the waves of storm that swept upon him. Turning into the wind was like going up a steep hill. Turning away from it was like lurching down a slope.

After a second or third circle he gave up hope, and yet he kept on looking for a sign of her. His eyes saw only splinterings and watery breakings of the torchlight now; they were so filled with fine silt. Then a ghost stepped into the patch of the ray, and it was the girl.

The wind whipped her hair forward into a ragged fluttering of light about her face, and she came on with one hand held out, feeling her way. She thought Mortimer was Sam Pearson and she stumbled on toward the light, crying out, 'Sam! God bless you, dear old Sam! I knew you were my last chance. But I thought ... never could find ...'

The wind blew her words to tattered phrases. It had reddened her eyes like weeping. 'Hampton – beautiful – gone –' she was saying.

The wind thrust her into his arms. She let herself go. There was no strength in all of her except the hands to hold on. He turned and made a windbreak for her. The storm lifted his bandanna from the back of his neck with deliberate malice. The flying sand pricked his skin

with a million needle points. Sometimes the drift
came bucketing at him out of scoop shovels with a
force that staggered him on his planted feet. He
had to hold up the girl, too. She was a good
weight. He thought of a loose sack with a hundred
and twenty-five pounds of Kansas wheat in it.
That was why she had a right to despise him,
because there was no poet in him. He ought to be
thinking of two souls who clung to each other in
this wild deluge, this ending of the world. She
said, 'I would have gone crazy with fear. But I
kept on tying to the thought of you, Sam.'

He had to tell her at once that he was not Sam
Pearson, but he could not tell her. He was a thief
stealing this moment out of her life, a guilty but
inexpressible happiness. The flashlight showed
the dust leaping past them, giving a face to the
scream of the wind.

She said, 'Father, if he guessed where I was,
would simply go plunging out and be lost. But I
thought of you, Sam, making up your mind slowly,
coming slowly. I knew you wouldn't want to waste
all the time you've put in teaching me things. And
I knew you'd find me ... God bless you ... God bless
you ...'

'Don't say it,' said Mortimer.

His voice put the strength back into her. As her
body stiffened, he knew that it was the strength of
shock and horror. He turned the light so that it
struck upon their faces. No, it was not horror and

128

disgust that he saw, but a profound wonder. The wind kept whipping her hair out like a ragged moment of light in the darkness of the storm. She still held to him.

'*You* came for me?' she asked.

He wanted to bring her back closer into his arms. He wanted to tell her that it wasn't hard to find her; he could have found her in the steam of hell because there was an instinct that would always show him the way. But he couldn't say that. He had to be honest, like a damned fool.

'*You* came for me?' she had asked.

'Partly for you,' said Mortimer.

All at once she was a thousand leagues away from him though she had merely taken one step back.

'Take Chico. He'll pull us through,' said Mortimer, and helped her strongly up into the saddle.

He should have said something else. He should have made some gallant protestation, he knew. Now she was despising him more than ever, as a gross, stupid, grotesque fool; or as a brute who saved her life not for love or pity, but from a sheer grinding sense of duty. He felt that he had lost his chance and that it would never come to him again.

Chico was the captain of the voyage, for through the whirl his instinct clung to the trail; Mortimer clung to a stirrup leather and floundered on, hoping to God that his knees would not give way.

When the sand and flying silt he breathed had choked the wise old mule, he halted, with his head down. Then Mortimer would swab out the nostrils and wash out the mouth of Chico. Sometimes, as he worked, the light from the pocket torch showed him the wind-bleared face of the girl, like a body adrift in the sea. Death could not have taken her farther from him, he knew. Yet she seemed more desirable than ever.

It was not always thick darkness. Sometimes the sky cleared a little, as long rents tore through the whirling explosions of dust, and then by daylight they saw the immensity of the clouds that rolled through the upper heavens and dragged their skirts along the ground.

They had gone on for hours when Mortimer, floundering through a darker bit of twilight, jostled heavily against Chico. The girl halted the mule and stood on the ground offering the reins and the saddle to Mortimer. He was staggering with weariness, but this proffer seemed to him an insulting challenge to his manhood. For answer, he picked her up and pitched her, like a child, high into the saddle. A sweep of the flashlight showed her face saying angry words which the wind blotted out.

Then they went forward again, with the anger clean gone from him. He could see now, in retrospect, that it had been merely a most gallant gesture on her part, but he had been as drunk with fatigue as he was heartsick now.

130

An age of desperate struggle followed, with his knees turning to water under his weight; and then something cried above him in the wind. It was the girl, pointing. He was able to see, though blurred and dimly, the outlines of Poplar Springs immediately before them!

A moment later they were in the town, they were approaching a light, a door was opening, they were entering a heavenly peace, with the hands of the storm removed and the voice of the storm increasing far away.

He lay on his back on the floor, coughing up black mud and choking on it. A young lad swabbed off his face, and said, 'Your eyes are terrible. I never seen such eyes. Don't it hurt terrible even to wink? Can you see anything?'

'Get that mule into shelter and water him, will you?' said Mortimer.

'He's fixed up already,' answered the lad.

Mortimer groaned and stretched out his arms crosswise. The great fatigue was flowing with a shudder out of his body; the hard floor soaked it up. He closed his eyes. Afterward there were a thousand things to do. This was the rest between rounds and then the hardest part of the fight was to come.

He heard a woman's voice cry out from another room, 'They're from the Chappany! They've come clear down the Chappany! This is Louise Miller!'

Someone jumped across the room toward

Mortimer. He opened his burning eyes and saw a man with a cropped gray head leaning over him and shaking a finger in his face. 'You didn't come down the Chappany!' he shouted. 'Did you come down the Chappany through all that hell?'

'We came down the Chappany,' said Mortimer.

'Bud, I'll take care of him. You run get Mr. Sloan and Pop Enderby and Jiggs Dawson and tell 'em they're going to hear what's happening in the Chappany. If it's blowin' away, Poplar Springs is gunna dry up and fade out. We don't live on nothing much but the Chappany trade.'

Mr. Sloan, the banker, and Enderby, the big cattleman, and Dawson, of the General Store, were only three among thirty when Mortimer sat up to face the crowd that poured into the house. They looked at big Mortimer in a painful silence, those thirty men who were packed across one end of the room. The front door kept opening and people stamped in from the storm, and hushed their footfalls when they saw what was in progress. Now and then the voice of the storm receded and Mortimer could hear the painful, excited breathing of those people in the hall.

Nobody talked except Oliver Sloan, the banker, and he was the only one of the visitors who sat down. He was a huge, wide man with a weight of sagging flesh that seemed to be exhausting his vital forces. In that silence he asked the questions and Mortimer answered.

132

'How's it look in general?'

'Bad,' said Mortimer.

'Hear from the Starrett place?'

'Yes. It's a sand-heap.'

'Over by Benson's Ford?'

'Don't you get any telephone messages?' asked Mortimer.

'All our lines are down. Hear from over by Benson's Ford?'

'I heard yesterday. The only thing that's left over there is hardpan.'

Half a dozen men drew in long breaths, drinking up that bad news. In Poplar Springs lived retired ranchers from all over the range.

'What about McIntyre's?' asked Sloan.

'The sand is fence-high,' said Mortimer.

'The Hancock place ... that's your own place, isn't it?'

'The soil is holding there. It's only going in spots,' said Mortimer.

'That's your work,' said the banker wearily. 'You said that you'd button down the topsoil; and you've done it?'

'I've done it,' said Mortimer. He broke out: 'I wish to God I could have helped the whole range. I wish I could have taught them. It's a poor happiness to me to save my own land and see the rest go up in smoke.'

No one said anything until the banker spoke again. He paid no attention to Mortimer's last protestation. 'Jenkins' place?' he asked.

'Those hills sheltered that land pretty well,' said Mortimer, 'but the sand is spilling over the edge of the hills and gradually covering the good soil.'

'See Crawford's?'

'Fence-high with drift.'

'The Grand ranch?' asked Sloan. He looked up with desperate eyes at Mortimer.

'I'm sorry,' answered Mortimer slowly.

'It's gone, is it?' whispered the banker.

'Hardpan,' said Mortimer.

Sloan pushed himself up out of his chair. How many of his mortgages were on mere heaps of blow-sand or hardpan acres, no one could tell; but from the ruin in his face the crowd pushed back to either side and let him out into the hall.

Mortimer called after him, 'But there's two thirds of the Chappany still holding. The worst of it there is that the water holes are silted up; even Miller's lakes are gone; and Charles Hancock won't let the cows come to his water. Cattle out there by the thousands are going to die. Is there any way of persuading Jim Hancock to give his son orders to let those cattle in to water?'

'Persuade him?' shouted Sloan. 'By God! I'll wring the orders out of his withered old neck with my own hands! Persuade him! We'll take the hide off his back, and see if that will persuade him!'

The whole mob poured out from the house;

among the rest, Mortimer had one glimpse of the
pale face of Lou Miller, and then she was lost in
the crowd. They moved into the street. They
flowed against the rush of the dust storm into the
General Merchandise Store of Poplar Springs.

To Mortimer's watery eyes the whole store was
like a scene under the sea. A score of men lounged
around the stove, retaining the winter habit in the
midst of the hot weather. There was constant
coughing, for the fine dust which was adrift in the
air constantly irritated the throats of the men. In
a corner two very old men leaned over a checker
game, one with a fine flow of white hair and beard,
and the other as bald and red as a turkey gobbler,
with a hanging double fold of loose red skin
beneath the chin. He gripped with his toothless
gums a clay pipe, polished and brown-black with
interminable years of use. He was Jim Hancock.
In his two years on the ranch, Mortimer had seen
him only once before.

'You talk to him first,' said Sloan.

Mortimer walked toward the players. Someone
near the stove muttered, 'See the eyes of *that* one?
Looks like those eyes had been sandpapered.'

'What will you say to him?' whispered the girl at
the side of Mortimer.

He gave no answer but, stepping to the table,
said, 'Sorry to interrupt you, Mr. Hancock, but ...'

'If you're sorry for it, don't do it,' said Jim
Hancock.

Ben Chalmers, the time-tried opponent of old Hancock, lifted his eyes and his hand from the checkerboard. He stared briefly at the interloper, and dragged his hand slowly down through his beard as he returned his attention to the game.

'Do you remember me, Mr. Hancock?' persisted Mortimer.

'I never heard of nobody I less remembered,' said Hancock, without looking up.

'I'm Mortimer, from your place on the Chappany,' said he.

'Then why don't you stay there?' asked Hancock.

'Miller's lakes are choked with sand.'

'I wish Miller was laying choked in one of 'em,' said Hancock.

'The water holes all over our part of the range are silted up, and so are most of the tanks. There's a water famine. Cows are going to die by thousands unless they can get water,' explained Mortimer.

'Cows have died by the thousands many a time before this,' replied Hancock.

'Thousands and thousands of cattle are milling around the fence between the Miller place and your two lakes,' said Mortimer.

'Let 'em mill and be damned,' answered Hancock.

'More than cattle will be damned,' stated Mortimer.

136

Hancock jerked up his head at last. 'D'you see me playing a game of checkers, or don't you? Is a man gunna have a little peace in the world, or has he gotta be hounded into his grave by fools like you?'

'The men who own the cattle ... they won't stand by and see them die of thirst. They'll cut the wire of the fences and let them through. It means gun fighting,' said Mortimer.

'Let 'em cut, then,' said Hancock. 'What do I care?'

'Charlie is out with his cowpunchers and rifles to keep those cows back,' the voice of Louise Miller said. 'He intends to shoot.'

Mortimer turned to her. She had sifted through to the front of the crowd.

'I hope he don't miss, then,' said Jim Hancock. 'Charlie always was a boy that wasn't worth nothing except when it comes to a fight. But, when it comes to a pinch, he's the out-fightingest son-of-a-gun that I ever seen. Now shut up, Lou, and don't bother me no more.'

Mortimer cried out, 'If the fight starts, there are two hundred armed men to take care of Charlie and his boys. They'll wash over them. A dozen men may die, but Charlie's sure to be one of them!'

'I hope he is,' answered Jim Hancock. 'It'll save a lot of rum for decent people if Charlie dies now.'

Mortimer moved suddenly with a gesture of surrender. Sloan, the banker, stepped in beside him, and remarked, 'I'll try my hand.... Jim, there's been damned near enough grazing land wiped off the range to ruin Poplar Springs; and if the cattle die this town'll ruin mighty fast. There's nobody but you can give the cows a second chance, without there's a war. Are you going to sit there and let everything go to hell?'

In place of an answer in words, old Jim Hancock reached back to his hip, produced a long-barreled, single-action forty-five, and laid it on his lap. Then he returned to his contemplation of his next move, merely saying, 'Sorry there's been all this damn' palavering, Ben.'

'I don't care what you're sorry about,' said Ben. 'You're spoilin' the game with all this fool talk.'

Another man from the crowd began to shout at old Jim Hancock with a loud voice, but Mortimer had seen enough. He felt sick and weak and utterly defeated. He jerked the door open and went across the street, leaning his body aslant into the thrust of the wind, to Porson's saloon. In the vacant lot beside it the tarpaulin cover which housed a caterpillar tractor flapped and strained like clumsy wings trying to take flight in the wind.

In the saloon he found only two dusty cowpunchers who stood at one end of the bar. Old Rip Porson, himself, leaned in an attitude of profoundly gloomy thought in front of his cracked mirror. He put out the bottle and tall glass for Mortimer's Scotch and soda.

138

'Ain't I seen you before?' asked Rip.

'Once or twice,' agreed Mortimer.

'You wasn't connected with mirror-busting, a while back, was you?' asked Porson. His angry, birdlike eyes stared into Mortimer's face. 'Because,' said Porson, 'there was thirteen high-power skunks in here, along with one man.'

'That's him, Rip,' said one of the cowpunchers. 'I reckon that's Mortimer, that done the kicking, and the others were them that were kicked.'

'Are you him?' said Rip Porson, sighing. 'I was kind of half hoping that I'd have a chance to open up and speak the mind that's in me to one of them low-down hounds. There used to be *men* on this range, but now there ain't nothing but legs and loud talk, and no hands at all,' said Rip Porson, tipping two fingers of whisky into a glass and tossing it off. 'Now we gotta import strangers like you. So here's to you, and drink her down.'

He sloshed more whisky into the glass and tossed it off. Instead of taking a chaser, he opened his mouth and took one long, panting breath.

Somewhere through the storm came the lowing of a cow, as though she mourned for her calf, and Mortimer's eye wandered as he thought of the milling thousands of foredoomed cattle up the Chappany. A bowl of fresh mint sprigs that stood behind the bar caught his eye, with its suggestion of that green and tender spring which would not come again to such a great portion of the range.

139

He thought, also, of that stubborn old Jim Hancock, all leather, without blood or heart.

'Can you mix the sort of julep that really talks to a man's insides?' asked Mortimer.

'Me? Can I mix a julep?' asked Rip Porson. 'I don't give a damn what time of year it is, the fellow that drinks my mint julep knows it's Christmas.'

'Build me a pair of them, then,' said Mortimer. 'Build them long and build them strong.' And he laughed a little, feebly, as he spoke. A moment later he was carrying the high, frosted glasses into the General Merchandise Store. For, when he remembered how the whisky in the barroom had relaxed his own troubles, it came to him, very dimly, that perhaps even the iron-hard nature of Jim Hancock might be altered a little.

As he went in, Sloan was going out, with a gray, weary face. He looked at Mortimer with unseeing eyes and passed on; but the remainder of the crowd was packed thick around the checker game where old Jim Hancock, with the revolver on his lap, still struggled through the silent fight against Ben Chalmers. Each had five crowned pieces. Mortimer put down the drinks at the right hand of each player and stepped back.

'It's no good,' said a sour-faced man. 'You can't soften up that old codger. There ain't any kindness left in him.'

The hand of Ben Chalmers left its position

beneath his chin, extended, wavered for a moment in the air, seized on a piece, and moved it. Continuing in the same slow, abstracted manner, the hand touched the glass, raised it, and tipped the drink at his lips. Jim Hancock, stirred by the same hypnotic influence, lifted his glass at the same time. Hancock put down his drink with jarring haste.

'Rye!' he exclaimed, making a spitting face. 'Rye!'

'I disrecollect,' said Ben Chalmers slowly, 'but seems like I *have* heard about folks ignorant enough to make a mint julep with Bourbon.'

'Ignorant?' queried Jim Hancock.

'Ignorant,' said Chalmers.

'There's only one state in the Union where a mint julep is made proper,' declared Jim Hancock. 'And that's Kentucky.'

'The Union be hanged,' said Ben Chalmers, 'but the only state is Virginia.'

'Kentucky,' said Jim Hancock.

'Virginia,' said Chalmers.

'Have I been wastin' my time all these years with an ornery old fool that don't know good whisky from bad?' demanded Hancock.

'You come from too far west to know good whisky from bad,' said Chalmers. 'When I think of a man of your years that ain't come to an understanding of a right whisky ...'

'East of Louisville, a right whisky ain't made,'

said Hancock. 'I'm drinkin' to Kentucky and the bluegrass, and to the devil with points east and north ...' He took a long drink of the mint julep and made another face.

'In points east of Kentucky,' said Ben Chalmers, 'this here country got its start. When Washington and the immortal Jefferson was doing their stuff, Kentucky was left to the wild turkeys and the Indians.'

'The breed run out in Virginia,' said Jim Hancock. 'They still got some pretty women, but the men went to Kentucky about a hundred years ago.'

'An outrage and a lie!' said Ben Chalmers.

He pushed himself back with such violence that the table rocked to and fro. The kings on the checkerboard lost their crowns and shuffled out of place as Ben Chalmers rose.

'A Virginia gentleman,' said Ben Chalmers, 'wouldn't go to Kentucky except to spit!'

'Who said Virginians were gentle and who said that they were men?' asked Jim Hancock, rubbing his chin with his fist.

Ben Chalmers uttered an inarticulate cry, fled to the door and through it, into the twilight of the storm outside.

'It *is* a great state, that Kentucky,' suggested Mortimer.

'Son,' said Jim Hancock, 'maybe you ain't quite the damn' fool that I been making you out.

Kentucky is the only state in the country where they breed men and hosses right.'

'They breed horses and men with plenty of bone and blood and nerve,' suggested Mortimer.

'They do,' said Hancock.

'Which is why nobody can understand why you're afraid to go back up the Chappany and keep Charlie from killing a dozen men or so and winding up with a rope around his neck,' continued Mortimer.

'Afraid? Who said afraid?' demanded Hancock, jumping up from the table.

'Shake hands on it, then, and we'll go together as soon as the storm gives us a chance,' invited Mortimer.

'Damn the storm! Why should we wait for the storm to give us a chance?' asked Hancock.

Beyond the window, dimly through the rush and whirl of the dust, Mortimer saw the tarpaulin which covered the caterpillar tractor flapping in the wind like a bird awkwardly tied to the ground. Nothing in the world could move like that caterpillar, through all weathers, over all terrain.

'Who owns that caterpillar?' he asked, pointing.

'It's mine,' said the manager of the General Store.

'Let me rent it to go up the Chappany,' said Mortimer.

'Rent it? I'll give it to you!' cried the manager. 'And, by God, there's nothing else that will take you where you want to go!'

The big machine was ready for use, with a full tank of gas; and the engine started at a touch. Mortimer tried the controls, rear, left, and centre, and the machine answered readily to the levers. Old Jim Hancock, thoroughly equipped with goggles, huddled himself into as small a space as possible on the floorboards. They started without ceremony. A great outbreak of shouting from the crowd seemed to Mortimer only a farewell cheer. He waved his hand in answer and shoved the tractor against the full sweep of the wind. He had full canteens of water and old Jim Hancock on board, and that was all he asked for, except the entire ten miles an hour that the caterpillar could make. That ten miles, added to the cutting edge of the wind, blew the dust right through the wet bandanna that masked him, nose and mouth; it blew the fine dust down to the bottom of his lungs.

Well, there is dust pneumonia also. He thought of that as the machine hit a five-foot sand drift and went through it part climbing, part awallow, with a flag of dust blowing and snapping behind it.

They entered the wide mouth of the Chappany Valley as the tractor put its nose into the soft of a bog, a water hole entirely clogged by drifted silt. Mortimer was backing out of this when a masked figure came up beside him, staggering, with outreaching hands.

He knew who it was. He knew instinctively, with a great stroke of the heart. He stopped the caterpillar clear of the bog, pulled Lou Miller into the machine, and put her on the floor. She must have ridden on the bucking, pitching tail of the tractor all the way from Poplar Springs, with the choking torrents of its own dust added to the blind onpouring of the storm. She was almost stifled, now, as he pulled down her bandanna and flashed his torch into a face begrimed and mud-caked to the eyes. Half a canteen squirted over her rinsed her white again, but she still lay gasping. He put his lips to her ears and called, 'Your lungs ... are they burning up? Can you get your breath?'

'I'm all right. Go on!' she answered.

'I'm turning back to Poplar Springs,' he answered.

She caught his arm with both hands and shook it. 'If you turn back, I'll throw myself out of the tractor,' she cried to him desperately. 'Go on! Go on! Think of what's happening up the Chappany!'

'Ay, go on! Go on!' yelled old Jim Hancock with a sudden enthusiasm.

Mortimer went on. The wind-beaten lights of the machine showed him a ten-foot sand drift, curving at the top like a wave about to break. He put on full speed and crashed through it. Sand flowed like heavy water over the entire tractor. He was blinded utterly, but the vibration of the racing caterpillar bucketed out the cargo of sand swiftly, like water. If the fine dust did not get to the bearings, and if the motor was not choked, they might get through.

Another sand wave heaved vaguely before him. He headed at full speed for it, straightening the nose of the caterpillar like the head of a spear for a target....

Far up the Chappany the murk of the day's end had joined the shadow of the storm, and with the coming of the thicker darkness John Miller prepared for the final action. While there was even a flicker of daylight to give the rifles of Charlie Hancock opportunity to aim he would not let his men move forward, but now the night had thickened the air of the valley to soup.

A floundering horse with a rider bent forward along its neck came by, the rider yelling, 'Miller! Hi, Miller!'

'Here!' shouted Miller, and the rider turned in toward him.

He leaned out to grip the pommel of Miller's saddle, and coughed and choked for a moment, head down, before he could speak. Miller took him by the shoulders and shouted at his ear, 'Shorty, was she at the Grimes place? Did you find her at Hogan's? Is there any word?'

'Gone!' gasped Shorty. 'Dave Weller come in and says she ain't at Parker's neither. There ain't no word.'

'The storm has her,' said Miller.

He pulled up his bandanna and spat down-wind. But he could breathe no better after that.

'There's twenty-one years of my life gone,' said John Miller. 'And God be kind to her ...' He gave the word to attack, then. The men were eager for action.

They had waited long enough, they felt, and the great, mournful song of the thirsty cattle was maddening to their ears. The whole throng of ranchers and cow hands poured into the Chappany.

They came with enthusiasm and a determination to rush Charlie Hancock and his men off the face of the earth, but when they put their eyes on the actual field of battle, some of their enthusiasm left them. Near the edge of the Hancock lake a flat-topped mesa jumped up a hundred feet above the valley floor. To climb the boulders and flat walls of the mesa was hard work, even in full daylight without the burden of a gun; to clamber up the height through these streaks of dark and light, with a rifle to manage and good marksmen taking aim from above, looked very bad work, indeed. If the storm had offered complete darkness, they could have fumbled through the safe darkness and grappled with Hancock and his men, but now the sky was half the time covered and half the time lighted through rents and explosive openings. Those gleams were sufficiently frequent

147

to give Hancock's riflemen an excellent chance to command the approaches to their rock.

Miller sent some of his people to climb the bluff above the lake, but when they reached the high land they were able to make out only glimpses of the men among the rocks; and the distance was too great for any sort of accurate shooting. Some of the ranchers wanted to cut the fences and let the cattle go trooping down to water, anyway, but it was readily pointed out to them that Hancock would enjoy nothing more than a chance to practice marksmanship on dumb cattle before he started on human targets.

It was a clumsy impasse. The storm kept bringing them the dolorous chorus of the cattle. They knew the cows were dying momently, going down from weakness and trampled by the milling herd. That was why Miller's crowd wanted blood and wanted it badly, but no one wanted to lead the rush against that impregnable rock.

There was a big rancher named Tucker Weed among Miller's following, a fellow with a voice as loud as that of a champion hog-caller from Missouri. It was he who raised a sound as shrilling as a bugle call and drew the attention of everyone to a pair of lights that staggered up the valley into the breath of the storm.

'What is it?' yelled Tucker Weed. 'It ain't an automobile. No automobile could head into this smother. What is it? It ain't the old red-eyed devil come looking for us, is it?'

John Miller saw the lights disappear, then reflect dimly on the whirl of the storm as the light pointed straight at the sky.

'It's something that knows a fence when it finds one,' said Miller. 'It's hit a fence with a sand drift backed against it.... What can it be?'

The two lights swerved down again, pointed at the earth, and then wavered out into the level of the valley, approaching the huge, melancholy sea-sound of the bellowing cattle. It ran straight for only a moment, however, and then swerved to the left and headed for the rock of Charlie Hancock....

The mourning chorus of the cattle behind the Miller fences had been with them for miles, but now, in a greater burst of light, as the black of the sky opened in a wide central vent, they could see the living acres that milled beyond the fences.

Old Jim Hancock stood up to see, and Mortimer steadied him by gripping his coat at the small of the back.

'Why, damn my old heart and eyes!' said Jim Hancock. 'Why didn't you tell me there was so many thirsty cows up here on the Chappany?'

It made no difference that he *had* been told. They had a demonstration of another sort a moment later when half a dozen young steers, finding some low place in the fence or, more likely, climbing over dead bodies that gave them a take-off to jump the wire, came clear of the fences and rushed at a gallop toward the water of the lake. The leader, after half a dozen strides, bucked into the air, landed on his nose, and lay still. Another and another dropped. From the top of the rock beside Hancock Lake little sparks of light showed where the rifles were playing. The half-dozen steers lay dead long, long before they brought their thirsty muzzles near the water.

'There he is!' shouted Jim Hancock. 'There's that doggone boy of mine, up there and raising hell. Good shooting, Charlie! Good shooting, old feller! ... But, by God, I'm gunna make you wish you'd never seen a gun!'

A sweep of horsemen poured suddenly about him out of the night. As he saw the masked faces and the guns, Mortimer brought the caterpillar to a halt. The cowpunchers were thick around them in an instant, and a voice was yelling, 'It's the dirt doctor and old poison-face Jim Hancock himself ... and there's Lou Miller, as much alive as you and me ...'

There was Miller, himself, at the side of the machine; and now Lou was in his arms, while Jim Hancock piped, 'Clear away from us. Leave me get at that Charlie fool of mine. I'm gunna teach him what comes of spoiling good beef when he ain't hungry.'

Someone reached in and smote the shoulder of

150

Mortimer; someone shouted, 'Great work, old-timer!' And then the crowd was drawn back and he shoved the caterpillar on toward the rock through a moment of darkness that swallowed the entire picture instantly. The headlights sometimes showed the way a hundred feet ahead; sometimes the brilliant cone choked off a stride away and they were charging blindly into the smoke and smother of the wind; then the zenith split open and light rushed back over the Chappany. They were under the great rock. They were not fifty paces from the rising wall, when a whole volley of bullets struck them. The headlights went out. One of the endless tracks stopped. The caterpiller began to turn clumsily.

Mortimer caught at old Hancock and with him dropped to the floor of the tractor as he shut off the engine. 'Are you hurt, Jim?' he asked.

'Hell, no!' said Hancock. 'But I guess they've shot a leg off this old horse of ours.'

The plunging rain of bullets still rang about them until that open funnel of brilliant sky above them misted over and then closed suddenly with a river of black.

'Will you go on with me, Jim?' shouted Mortimer. 'Will you try to climb up to them with me and talk to Charlie?'

'Don't be a damn' young fool,' said Jim Hancock. 'I'll go alone. Why should you let 'em get at you with their guns?'

But Mortimer went with him. He hooked his arm around the hard, withered body of the old man and fairly dragged him through the blind current of the storm until they found the loom of the rock, and then, suddenly, the wall itself. They paused there a moment, gasping, coughing as though they had just escaped from the smoke of a burning house. Then they started up. The big boulders at the foot of the wall offered stepping-stones to begin with, but above them came almost a sheer rise. They had to wait for the next break in the windy darkness of the sky before they could continue, taking advantage of a fissure here and a projection there. Mortimer, keeping just below, helped the old fellow strongly up while Hancock muttered, 'I'll fix him ... beef butcher! ... damn' fool! ...'

They were well up the rock when guns crackled above them rapidly, like pitchpine burning. A bullet streaked a white scar across the rock in front of Mortimer's face; another raked him through the back muscles with an exquisite stroke of agony; then a fist-stroke and knife-thrust combined lanced him in the side. He had a good handhold on a projecting spur of rock, so he managed to keep his place; and when old Hancock dropped, suddenly, he managed to catch him by the coat and hold him swinging out over empty space, though that effort cost him nearly the last of his strength.

A mercy of the wind closed up the gap in the sky, at that moment; and in the darkness the gunfire ended.

Old Jim, agile as a dried-up tomcat, went clawing up the rock, screeching, 'Charlie! Charlie! You double-jointed jackass! Put down them guns or I'll ...'

Mortimer followed the inspired fury of the old fellow, but his strength was running out of him. The light came back a moment later and made him shrink as though it had been the flash of a knife. And then he saw Jim Hancock standing on the lip of the rock above him, shaking one fist above his head. Men loomed beside him. The soft bulk of Charlie Hancock appeared. And Mortimer drew himself up to the flat top of the mesa. When he got there, he had to lie out flat. The pain left his side and burned only in his brain.

He could hear Jim Hancock shouting, 'Get down there! I hope they drill you full of lead when you come to 'em, begging, with your hands up. Get down there and tell 'em to open the fences up and let the cows through! Save your damned face if you can – tell 'em it was a joke! Your ma died for you, and, damn you, you been nothing but a long, cold winter to me all your life. Get out of my sight!' ...

There seemed to be light still in the sky, but a darkness crawled out of Mortimer's brain and covered his eyes.

After a time he saw that he was lying near a fire that burned behind a screen of boulders at the top of the mesa. A withered forearm with a bandage around it appeared in his line of sight. A hand lifted his head.

'Take a shot of this,' said Jim Hancock, holding a whisky flask at his lips.

He got down a good, long swallow of the stuff. It burned some of the torment away.

Jim Hancock said, 'You take the rest.... If you die, I'm gunna have 'em hanged, every damn' one of 'em ... and we won't wait for the law, neither.'

'No,' said a big voice. 'We won't wait for no law!'

That was Jan Erickson. And there were others of the gang watching their chief with grimly set faces.

'Yes, sir,' said Jim Hancock, 'if you pass out, we're gunna string 'em up, and I'll help pull on the ropes. So you rest nice and easy.'

It was an odd way of giving comfort. Mortimer tried to laugh a bit, but fingers of pain seemed to tear him half apart.

'I'm gunna lift up your head and leave you have a look at what's happening,' said Hancock.

Accordingly, slowly and carefully he lifted Mortimer's head and shoulders until he could look over the sloping top of the mesa and down into the valley of the Chappany at Hancock Lake. The waters of it seemed to have living shores until his eyes cleared a little and he could see the cattle ten and twenty deep as they drank up life and new strength.

'That's pretty good,' said Mortimer. 'I'm glad I saw that,' he said.

'Don't talk,' said Hancock. 'They've got you drilled right through the lungs, and talking is sure poison for you.'

The darkness, like living shadows in the corners of a room, began to crawl out over the eyes of Mortimer. If he were shot through the lungs, he had to die and he was sure that he was dying at that moment. 'I've got to talk,' he said.

'Shut your mouth!' commanded Hancock.

Mortimer forced out the words slowly: 'Tell Lou Miller it was never a joke. I loved her. Tell her I loved her, but I don't blame her for the way she felt....'

He seemed to be walking, then, through infinite darkness, opening doors, feeling his way down blank walls, finding more doors, opening them, and something was whistling to him far away. He opened his eyes. It was the scream of the storm that he had been hearing, but far withdrawn again into the heart of the sky.

He looked down at the big arch of his chest and the great bandage which was being unwrapped by slender hands, unlike the hands one finds on a cattle range. His lips were saying, 'Somebody promise to tell Lou Miller ...'

Someone leaned over him, saying, 'I know –

darling!'

Now, by an effort of peering into distance, he made out her face. She was much older. She was so drawn and white and old that, to any ordinary eye, half of her beauty was surely gone; but his eye alone, which knew how to see her, found her far more beautiful than ever.

His breast lay bare as a voice said, 'Don't let him talk.'

'Make him stop talking, Lou,' said Miller's voice out of the darkness.

She touched the lips of Mortimer, and he kissed her hand. If there were only a few moments left, words were no good, after all. Touching her and looking at her was all that mattered.

The crisp voice of command said, 'He's lost blood. He's lost buckets of blood, but I don't think … give me that probe.'

A finger of consummate pain entered his breast, his side, glided back.

'Certainly not!' said that voice of authority. 'The man has ribs like the ribs of a ship. And the bullet glanced around them.'

The darkness covered Mortimer's eyes with a sudden hand, but through the shadow he could hear the sudden, joyful outcry of the girl, fading out of his consciousness rapidly, but lodging somewhere in his heart the promise of life and of happiness. ✓

P